BOSS OF HER

ANNA STONE

ISBN: 9781922685193

BOOKS BY ANNA STONE

IRRESISTIBLY BOUND SERIES

Being Hers

Her Surrender

Hers to Keep

Freeing Her

MISTRESS SERIES

Tangled Vows

Ensnared Hearts

Forever Theirs

Guarded Desires

QUEENS SERIES

Capturing Tess

Saving Mia

BLACK DIAMOND SERIES (WITH HILDRED BILLINGS)

The Girlfriend Arrangement

The Executive Liaison

The Bodyguard Affair

STANDALONES

Behind Closed Doors

One Last Dance

"Why did I let you talk me into this?" Jade muttered, glancing down the line in front of them. At least it was shorter than the line behind them.

"Into what?" Renee ran her hands through her short, dark hair. "Having a little fun, for once?"

"I shouldn't be here. I should be getting ready for my interview."

"It's on *Monday*. You'll have all of Sunday to get ready. And knowing you, you've already spent the past week preparing."

Jade crossed her arms. "You don't understand how important this interview is. This isn't just any job. It's an executive assistant job for *Simone Weiss*."

Renee raised an eyebrow. "Am I supposed to know who that is?"

"Simone Weiss? LA's hotel queen? Owns half the hotels in the city?"

Renee stared back at her blankly.

"Let me put it this way. If I get this job, it'll open any

career door I want. Simone's name is enough to do that. And the kind of experience I'll get working for someone like her is priceless." Jade had already passed the preliminary interview. She was the final candidate. All that was left was the interview with Simone herself. "Opportunities like this don't come every day. I can't afford to screw it up."

"Opportunities like *this* don't come every day either. Do you have any idea how hard it was to get on the guest list for tonight? I had to talk to my ex, Jade. My *ex*."

"Which one?" Jade murmured. It was hard to keep track of all the women Renee dated.

"You know, the aspiring actress who ditched me as soon as she got her five minutes of fame? And now I owe *her* a favor. This better be worth it."

Jade glanced down the line again. It hadn't moved. "What's so special about this place anyway?"

"You'll see when we get inside," Renee said. "Just trust me on this."

"Well, I can't have a big night tonight. I couldn't afford it even if I wanted to."

For the past couple of years, Jade had survived on grad school grants, but now that she'd graduated, she had no money coming in. She'd been relying on what little savings she had to cover food and rent on her studio, but her bank account had run dry. She needed this job.

Renee slipped her hands into her pockets. "Don't worry about paying for anything tonight. Drinks are on me."

Jade studied her friend through narrowed eyes. "Okay, what's going on?"

"What do you mean?"

"Why are you being so generous? Why did you want me to come out with you so badly in the first place?"

"Because it's *opening night*. Opening night of a brand-new ladies-only club right here in West Hollywood. This is the hottest event on the sapphic social calendar this year!"

"Right," Jade said. "So why didn't you ask someone else to come with you? You know, someone who actually cares about things like 'the sapphic social calendar'?"

"Like who? Most of my other friends are as straight as they come."

"And here I thought you asked me because you want to spend time with me."

"That too," Renee said. "Come on, Jade. We haven't gone out like this since undergrad. I just want us to have some fun together like we used to. And maybe get you to loosen up a little. You're so high-strung these days."

Jade glanced to the side. "Yeah, well, a lot has changed since undergrad."

That was when she'd first met Renee. They'd been assigned roommates in their freshman year, and she was the first friend Jade made after moving to Los Angeles from her small midwestern town. They'd been inseparable throughout college, but they'd drifted apart in the years since. Or rather, Jade had drifted apart from most of her friends from college.

Renee put her hand on Jade's shoulder. "Just promise me you'll at least try to have fun tonight?"

"I will," Jade said. "After all, I should enjoy myself while I can. If I get this job, tonight will be my last night of freedom for a while."

Simone Weiss had a formidable reputation. If everything Jade had heard about her was true, Simone would expect her assistant to live and breathe her job. But that was exactly what Jade wanted.

Renee squeezed Jade's shoulder. "I know you're going to have a great time. Just keep an open mind, okay?"

Before Jade could ask her friend what she meant, the line in front of them started moving.

"Finally," Renee said. "Come on."

They reached the entrance to the club. Above it, a purple neon sign glowed, bearing the name of the venue.

"*Club Velvet*," Renee read. "Are you ready?"

Jade nodded. "Let's do this."

They stepped through the doors and into the lobby, where a woman in a black leather catsuit and stilettos greeted them. After checking their IDs, she handed them each a clipboard with a dozen pages to sign. Club rules. NDAs. Safety waivers.

Jade flicked through the pages. "This seems like overkill. What kind of club is this?"

Renee shrugged and scribbled her signature at the bottom of each page. Jade did the same, barely reading a word of what she signed. She was usually much more cautious. But Renee may have had a point about her needing to 'loosen up a little.'

They handed the clipboards back to the leather-clad woman, who nodded toward the doors leading into the club. "Go on in. Have fun and be safe."

Be safe? Jade didn't get the chance to dwell on the woman's words. The next thing she knew, Renee was dragging her into the club.

"Wow." Renee stopped inside the doors, looking around. "This place is *nice*."

Jade murmured in agreement, taking in their surroundings. The club was packed and buzzing with electricity. Waitstaff dressed in black suits roamed through the crowd offering complimentary glasses of champagne to the guests, who lounged on plush leather seating or stood around the small dance floor. The neon lighting paired with black and purple damask wallpaper and lavish furnishings should have clashed. Instead, it gave the club an air of elegance and luxury.

"Yeah, this was worth talking to my ex for," Renee said. "And getting all dressed up for."

To Renee, getting "all dressed up" meant a pair of black chinos and a dark button-up shirt. Jade had gone with her favorite dress, a black and silver number that showed off her curves rather than swallowing them up like most clothes designed for women with her figure did. She'd paired it with low heels and silver drop earrings, and she'd left her hair loose.

And while half of the crowd was dressed just like them, the other half wore clothes that were less conventional. Corsets. Lingerie. Leather, and lots of it. A woman nearby wore a collar with a matching leather mask that covered almost her entire face, with ears like a fox. Attached to the collar was a leash, the other end held by a woman in a latex bodysuit.

Jade frowned. She'd lived in Los Angeles for years now. She was used to people wearing unusual outfits, all in the name of fashion. But this? This was something different.

"Renee?" Jade grabbed her friend's arm. "Just what kind of club did you bring me to?"

"Uh, right." Renee glanced around furtively. "So, I might have forgotten to mention that this isn't *just* a ladies-only club. It's a ladies-only *BDSM club*."

And just like that, everything fell into place. Renee telling her to keep an open mind. All the documents they'd had to sign just to set foot inside. The woman at the door in a leather catsuit. No, she wasn't sporting some hot new fashion trend Jade was unaware of. Neither was anyone else in the club.

"How could you not tell me something like that?" Jade hissed.

Renee shrugged. "I knew you wouldn't come if I did."

"Yeah, and you were right about that."

"Well, you're here already, so…"

Jade held up her hands, palms out. "No. No way."

"Come on," Renee said. "We waited in line for so long to get in. You might as well stay."

"And what? Watch people have sex?"

"That's not what this place is about. This isn't a sex club. Kink isn't just sex, it's—" Renee sighed. "Look, this is just the opening night party. It's about drumming up buzz and giving people a taste of what the club has to offer. There's no sex allowed. Not tonight, anyway."

Jade eyed two women making out in the corner nearby. One had the other pinned against the wall, her hand creeping up the other woman's thigh underneath her skirt.

"Maybe those two didn't get the message," Renee said.

Jade shook her head. "Why do you want me to stay, anyway? Why do you even want to be here?"

"Isn't it obvious?"

Jade blinked. "You mean, you're into this kind of thing?"

"Well, yeah. It's the real reason I wanted to come here tonight."

"Oh. I guess I didn't know that about you."

"Look, I know this probably isn't your thing. You're not the most adventurous, or the most experienced."

Jade scowled. She didn't need Renee to remind her of that.

"But aren't you even a little curious?"

Jade looked around the room. *Was* she curious about all this?

"You don't have to answer that," Renee said. "Even if you aren't interested, will you at least stay a little while? You know, keep me company?"

Jade studied Renee's face. Was this her friend's way of telling her she was nervous about being here alone? Renee would never admit something like that.

And maybe she had a point. Maybe Jade was a bit high-strung. Maybe she did need to have some fun.

Maybe she was a little *curious*.

"What the hell," Jade said. "I'll stay."

Renee smiled. "Great. Who knows, you might meet someone. Get a little action."

Jade rolled her eyes. "I don't think so."

"Come on, isn't it time you got laid?"

"I'm not as inexperienced as you think."

"Uh-huh. Do you have a secret girlfriend you never told me about?"

Not exactly. But Jade didn't want to think about *her* now. Or ever again.

"Like I said, just keep an open mind." Renee plucked two glasses of champagne from a passing server. "Here, a drink will help."

She handed a glass to Jade. Jade sipped it slowly, looking around the room. "I can't believe how many people are here. Who knew so many women were interested in, well, you know."

"Are you kidding? I can't remember the last time I slept

with a woman who didn't beg me to tie her up or spank her. But I have a type."

Warmth crept up Jade's face. She was used to Renee's uncensored comments about her sex life, but they still made her blush.

"It's about time we got a club like this in LA," Renee said. "I heard it was started by a bunch of rich lesbians to give women a place of our own to have fun and express ourselves. I can't wait to check out The Playroom."

"What's that?" Jade asked.

Renee grinned. "You'll see. Come on."

Champagne in hand, she led Jade to a large room off the main area of the club. Inside, half a dozen stations were scattered around. And at each station, a scene played out. In the corner, a woman kneeled inside a cage, dressed in an outfit that made lingerie look modest. Nearby, a curvy blonde lay bound to a bench as another woman drew her fingers along the backs of her thighs with one hand, a long, thin whip held in the other.

But that didn't prepare Jade for the woman who walked straight past them wearing nothing but a thong. Her torso was covered in crisscrossing ropes, forming intricate patterns over and around her breasts and stomach, the same ropes binding her hands behind her back.

Jade's skin began to burn. The woman was near naked, powerless to shield herself from those around her. But that didn't stop her from walking confidently through the crowd.

It was so twisted. So salacious.

So *thrilling*.

Renee grabbed hold of her arm, pulling her to the side. "You're blocking the doorway."

Jade blinked. "Right."

"Come on, let's go take a closer look."

Drinks in hand, they made their way around the room, watching scene after scene play out. They passed the woman in the cage, who seemed to be in a kind of blissful trance. They passed a woman cuffed spreadeagled to the wall like a piece of kinky art. Another woman stood before her, a finger hooked under the restrained woman's collar, teasing the inside of her thigh with the tip of a riding crop.

"Apparently, what's out here is nothing compared to the private rooms they have in the back," Renee murmured. "They aren't open yet, but I'm definitely coming back when they are."

But Jade barely heard a word Renee said. Because at that moment, her eyes fell on a scene playing out nearby. And before she could stop them, her feet carried her toward it.

In the center of the room, for all to see, was a naked woman suspended from a hook in the ceiling, thick, crimson ropes bound all around her body, a silken blindfold covering her eyes.

Beside her was another woman, a redhead dressed in a corset of velvet and lace, stiletto heels on her feet. She drew her hands along the bound woman's body, checking the knots, caressing bare flesh. As she ran her hands over the woman's cheek, whispered into her ear, the bound woman leaned her head against the redhead's chest, a soft purr rising from her. It was as if she was drunk, intoxicated by the redhead's touch.

Deep inside Jade's body, desire flickered and flared. *I'm not into this. Am I?*

She couldn't deny the rush that just watching the women gave her, the bound woman in particular. Blinded and immobilized, helpless and vulnerable, she was at the mercy of the other woman, of everyone in the room. She had no choice but to trust the redhead completely.

Why did the idea excite Jade as much as it terrified her?

Her heart thumped hard against the inside of her chest. Suddenly, the room was too stuffy, too crowded.

"I need to get out of here," she murmured.

Without waiting for Renee, she pushed through the crowd and made her way back to the main room. Her whole body was alight, her skin sizzling. And she'd downed the whole glass of champagne already, without even realizing it. Was that why her head was spinning?

"Hey." Renee's voice. She grabbed Jade's hand and pulled her into a quiet corner of the room. "What's wrong? Are you okay?"

"Yeah," Jade said. "It was just so hot and crowded in there. And that drink is really hitting me."

"Let me get you some water."

"You don't have to do that. I'm okay, really."

"I need another drink anyway. Are you going to be all right if I leave you alone for a second?"

Jade nodded. "Thanks, Ree."

As Renee headed for the bar, Jade drew in a few deep breaths, attempting to settle her racing heart. But couldn't silence the thrill deep within her body. She couldn't push images of the bound woman out of her mind. She couldn't help but wonder what that would feel like—

"What's someone as pretty as you doing here all alone?"

Jade tensed and looked up to find a dark-haired woman standing before her. She'd been so lost in her thoughts that she hadn't noticed her approach.

"I'm Tina, but you can call me Mistress T." The woman stepped closer. "And you are?"

"I'm—" Jade found her voice again. "I'm not alone. My friend is at the bar."

Jade glanced across the room. Renee was at the bar, all right. But she seemed less interested in ordering drinks and more interested in flirting with the woman beside her.

Tina's eyes followed hers to the bar. "Is that your friend? Looks like she's occupied." She turned back to Jade, a leering look in her eye that made Jade's skin itch. "So why don't the two of us get to know each other?"

Jade swallowed, her mouth suddenly dry. Why was she freezing up? She was the kind of person who thrived in high-pressure situations. Exams, job interviews, presentations—she could handle them in her sleep. So why was this woman turning her into a stammering mess?

Tina leaned in, not noticing—or caring—that Jade cringed back from her. "How about you and I go have some fun? The private rooms might be closed, but we can still play out here."

Jade took a step back, hitting the wall behind her. "I-I'm not interested."

"Don't play coy with me. You come here tonight, dressed in that sexy little number, and you're not up for having a little fun?" The woman put her hand on the wall next to Jade's head and leaned close, her alcohol-tinged breath hot on Jade's neck. "Come on, kitten. I know what you really want."

Jade's skin crawled. She didn't want this. All she wanted was this woman gone.

Her hands curled into fists at her sides. She straightened

up, looking the woman in the eye. "I said *no*. So leave me alone!"

The woman flinched. But a moment later, a smirk crossed her lips. "Oh, a feisty one. I like that even more."

Jade's stomach sank. This woman wasn't going to leave her alone. And she was taller than Jade, stronger than her, and they were in a darkened corner of the club, away from everyone else. Tina had her trapped. She couldn't move, couldn't breathe—

"Get away from her." A woman's voice, rising over the music and the hum of the crowd. "*Now.*"

CHAPTER 2

J ade's heart skipped. *That voice. Who?*

She looked over Tina's shoulder. Standing behind her was another woman, statuesque and commanding, her ice-blonde hair flowing down her shoulders. Diamond earrings adorned her ears, and she wore a short but elegant black dress with a deep V neckline, her ruby-red heels the same color as her lips.

And her eyes. In the dim light of the club, her amber eyes shone like gold, piercing into Tina.

Tina looked the blonde woman up and down, then cocked her head at Jade. "This your girl?"

"It doesn't matter if she is or not." That voice again, clear and sharp, cold as frost. "She said *no*. You understand what *no* means, don't you?"

Tina took a step back from Jade. "Look, lady—"

"It's a simple question. *No*. Do you understand the word?"

"Yes, but—"

The woman's gaze darkened. "Then why are you still here?"

Tina folded her arms across her chest. "Just who do you think you are?"

"Someone you don't want to cross. So I suggest you leave this club right now and never come back."

Tina scoffed. "Are you serious?"

"Do I look like I'm joking?"

Tina glanced between Jade and the other woman as if Jade would share her disbelief. But Jade only crossed her arms, saying nothing.

The blonde woman stepped between them, locking eyes with Tina in an unyielding glare.

"Leave," she said.

Tina stared back at her with narrowed eyes. Jade held her breath as neither woman moved or spoke.

Until Tina turned on her heel and walked away, pushing through the crowd and disappearing out the door to the club.

Jade let out a breath. Tina was gone. But in her place was the woman who had scared her off with nothing more than a few words and a look.

And right now, her gaze was fixed on Jade.

"Are you all right?" she asked.

Jade nodded. "Just a little flustered. She wouldn't leave me alone."

"What's your name?"

"It's Jade."

"Well, Jade, let me assure you that she will not bother you again. And she won't be allowed in here ever again, either."

Who was this woman and how did she have the power

to make that happen? Her voice was so confident and firm that Jade didn't doubt she did.

"Thank you. I'm not usually such a pushover, I just—" Jade shook her head. "I've been off-balance all night."

The woman gave her a sharp look. "*Do not* blame yourself for someone else's actions. You weren't being a pushover. She was being a predator, understand?"

Jade nodded, her cheeks growing warm. Why did this woman have her so hot and bothered? And why did she seem familiar, somehow? They couldn't have met before, because Jade would have remembered meeting somebody like her. Was she famous, then? It wasn't uncommon to run into minor celebrities in Los Angeles, and even the occasional major celebrity.

But the woman didn't seem like a celebrity. With her flawlessly styled hair, her finely tailored dress that was both classy and undeniably sexy at the same time, her unwavering confidence, she had an air of sophistication about her that seemed above the garishness of Hollywood.

"So what is it that has you off-balance tonight?" the woman asked. "You didn't look like you were having a good time even before she approached you."

Jade blinked. "You were watching me?"

"You didn't answer my question."

Jade's face grew even hotter. "I wasn't having a bad time. I just wasn't prepared for, well, *this*." She gestured toward the rest of the club. "My friend dragged me here tonight, and I didn't think I was into any of this, but now…"

Why was she admitting this to someone she'd only just met when she could barely admit it to herself? Why was she so calm when moments ago she'd barely been able to breathe? There was something about the woman that had

Jade mesmerized. And every time she spoke, it sent shivers trickling through her body.

"But now," the woman echoed, "your interest is piqued?"

Jade nodded.

"Then you've come to the right place. Have you had a look at The Playroom yet?"

"Yes," Jade replied.

"And what did you think of it?"

"It was… interesting."

The woman's ruby lips curled up in a slight smile. "Everything out here is just the tip of the iceberg. The private rooms are where the real magic happens. They're not open to the public yet, but I can get you inside."

Jade's pulse fluttered. Renee had told her about the private rooms. What was inside them?

"It would only be to have a look," the woman said. "Unless, of course, you wanted something more."

Jade bit her lip. "You mean…"

"I could show you the ropes, so to speak. Show you all the tantalizing things Club Velvet has to offer. And what *I* have to offer."

The woman leaned in close, her breath caressing Jade's cheek.

"Come with me," she whispered, "and I'll show you the exquisite pleasures submission can bring."

Jade's lips parted, a soft breath escaping them. She'd never been propositioned before. She wasn't the adventurous type. She didn't take risks, didn't let herself lose her inhibitions. And she definitely didn't have kinky trysts with women she'd just met. Especially not women who were older and far more sophisticated than her.

So why did the idea make her whole body throb? Why did she so desperately want to say *yes*?

"I..." Jade glanced to the side, breaking away from the woman's gaze. But as she did, she caught a glimpse of Renee walking toward her, a drink in each hand. When she noticed the woman standing with Jade, she stopped short, her eyes wide as she mouthed silently to Jade from a distance.

Go for it.

But all Renee did was bring Jade back to her senses. She shook her head. *What am I doing? What am I thinking?*

"Thanks for the offer," she said quickly. "But my friend is back. Maybe another time."

For a moment, Jade expected the woman would keep pushing her, just like Tina had.

But she only glanced in Renee's direction, then gave Jade a small nod. "I'll leave you to it. It was a pleasure meeting you, Jade."

Giving her one last piercing look, the woman turned and walked away. As she passed by Renee, she stopped and spoke a few words to her before disappearing into the crowd again.

And just like that, she was gone.

A few seconds later, Renee reached her. "Who was *that*?"

"She was no one." But Jade could still feel that woman's eyes on her, could feel the way her voice made her quiver and her gaze made her whole body burn.

"She was totally flirting with you. What happened?"

Jade shrugged. "I just wasn't interested."

"Is there something wrong with your eyes? She's hot as hell. And she looks like she knows how to bring a girl to her knees. That's not my thing, but I can appreciate it when I see it."

"Like I said, I'm just not interested." Jade paused. "What did she say to you just now, anyway?"

"Something about how I should do a better job of looking out for my friends, whatever that means."

"Oh god." Jade rubbed her temples. "I can't believe she said that to you."

"Did something happen?"

"It's a long story. But everything's fine now." Jade took the glass of water from Renee's hand and gulped the entire thing down. "Thanks for this, by the way."

"Whoa, are you sure you're okay?"

Jade nodded. "I'm great."

But her heart was still racing, along with her mind. This mysterious stranger had come along, effortlessly dispatched the other woman, and offered Jade a chance to explore the kind of wild fantasies she'd never even dreamed of until tonight.

And Jade had turned her down. Because trusting her, putting herself in the hands of another even for a moment, was too risky. She'd been naïve and trusting once upon a time, and she'd paid the price. That innocent girl was long gone. In her place was someone who knew better.

And Jade would never make the same mistake again.

CHAPTER 3

Simone folded her hands on the conference room table and locked eyes with the man across from her, speaking calmly.

"Is this some kind of joke, Gene?"

He exchanged a glance with the men sitting on either side of him, then crossed his arms, flashing the platinum Rolex on his wrist. "Is there a problem?"

Simone held back a sigh. She didn't have the patience for games. And she didn't have the patience for men like Gene Kingsley. The property magnate made a business of buying up land all over Los Angeles and sitting on it for years, decades even, leaving whatever was on it to rot, until he could sell it off for millions. He was exactly the kind of person she despised doing business with.

But he had something Simone wanted—a plot of land in Silver Lake, currently occupied by an abandoned motel. It was the perfect location for a luxury hotel. It was also the only part of Los Angeles that Simone didn't already have a hotel in, and Gene knew it.

He thought he had the upper hand. It was the only explanation for the dirty trick he was trying to pull.

"Don't play dumb with me, Gene. It's beneath you." Simone pushed the contract on the table before her away. "This? This isn't what we agreed upon."

Gene shrugged. "Sure, we talked terms. But until the ink is dry, it's all just that. Talk."

"We had an agreement," Simone said firmly. "A verbal agreement, but an agreement nonetheless. I made an offer. You accepted it. So why is the figure on this contract ten percent higher?"

"I changed my mind. That land is in a prime location. It's worth far more than what you're offering." He leaned back in his chair, a smirk crossing his lips. "Consider this my counter. I won't take a cent less."

Simone drew in a deep breath. She'd spent weeks negotiating with Gene, all in good faith.

She was done being civil.

"*Listen,*" she said. "You either sell me that land for the price we agreed upon, or you get the hell out of my conference room and never come back."

He held up his hands. "Settle down. Look, I'm open to negotiations. But your original offer—"

"That you accepted."

"Yes, but—"

"It's a fair price. We both know you're not going to get a better one."

"Maybe not right now. But in five years? That's a different story. So if you're not willing to up your offer, I'll take the land off the market and let time do the work."

Simone leaned back in her chair and crossed her arms.

"How's your wife, Gene?"

The man blinked. "My wife? She's fine. Why do you ask?"

"No reason. But you've sold off a significant portion of your company's assets recently and transferred the funds offshore. It's almost as if you're squirreling away your wealth so it can't be touched by anyone. A soon-to-be *ex*-wife, for example?"

His face paled. Gene Kingsley's rocky marriage was an open secret in certain circles. While Simone didn't enjoy the kind of banal conversation that went on at high-class parties, occasionally she'd glean a piece of information that was useful to her.

Like the fact that Gene's wife was planning to leave him and take him for half his worth. And rightfully so, given the rumors about the kind of husband he was. The fact that he was trying to sell off assets and hide the money in preparation? Simone had extrapolated that by herself.

And Gene's expression told her that her suspicions were correct. The man was desperate. He needed this sale even more than Simone did.

Anyone in her shoes would be tempted to use that to their advantage, to drop their offer to a fraction of what the plot was worth, knowing that Gene would have no choice but to accept it. And given his underhanded tactics, it was what he deserved.

But while Simone had a reputation for relentlessness, she refused to play dirty. Exploiting her competition made her no better than men like Gene.

"I don't care what's going on in your personal life," Simone said. "But your financial situation is no excuse to try to cheat me. I'm offering you a fair price. You know it. I know it. And frankly, after this stunt you pulled, I should walk away right now."

"Simone, just—"

"I am *not* finished." She rose from her seat, her fingers splayed on the table in front of her. "Despite what you tried to pull, despite you reneging on our agreement, I'm willing to hold up my end of the deal. So either sell me the land for what we agreed upon, or get out of my sight."

Silence fell over the room. Gene's smirk was long gone now. Instead, his lips were pressed firmly together, his hands balled up on the table.

He glanced at the men on either side of him. "I need a moment to confer with my lawyers."

"No, you won't be wasting any more of my time." Simone gathered her things from the table. "We're done here. I'll give you a moment, but I expect you out of this room, and this building, within the next ten minutes."

She marched toward the door. But she only made it a few steps before Gene stood up abruptly, knocking his chair over in the process.

"Fine!" he said. "I'll honor our agreement. The original agreement, that is. The plot is yours."

Simone paused, her back to him, for just long enough to make him sweat.

Then she turned and gave him a curt nod. "Then let's get that contract finalized before I change my mind."

Fifteen minutes later, she led Gene and his lawyers out of the conference room. "I'm glad we were able to come to an agreement," she said.

Gene murmured something inaudible. Simone ignored him. He could grumble and sulk all he liked. She'd gotten what she wanted.

But as they reached the elevator, she took Gene's hand and shook it firmly, leaning in and speaking quietly so only he could hear. "If you ever try anything like that again, I'll make sure you're blacklisted from every hotel on the West Coast."

Gene's face reddened. But Simone didn't let go of his hand. Not until the elevator arrived, and he nodded in acquiescence.

Once the men were gone, Simone made her way back to her office and shut the door behind her, taking a seat in the leather chair behind her desk. The large rosewood desk was an antique piece she'd acquired years ago, the very day she'd started her company. Like everything else in her office, from the gleaming marble floors to the Persian rug under the coffee table, she'd been drawn to its timeless elegance.

Even the building itself had the same charm to it, its original features kept in pristine condition over the years. It was why she'd chosen it for her company's office, which occupied the top two floors. She'd always favored things with history. Perhaps because she liked the idea of making history herself, of leaving an indelible mark on it.

She was already headed in that direction. She was only in her mid-thirties and she'd already made a name for herself, having been crowned Los Angeles' hotel queen. But she had bigger plans, bigger goals. And now that the deal with Gene was done, she could focus on acquiring her next prize.

The Ashton Star.

The prestigious five-star hotel was one of the oldest in Los Angeles, standing proudly at the heart of the city. And once Simone acquired it, it would be the crown jewel of her empire, embodying everything she'd worked for over the years.

She opened up her laptop. If she was going to make The Ashton Star hers, she couldn't afford to waste a single minute. She'd already started laying the groundwork, but she had plans to draft, meetings to arrange, connections to call upon. Her workday wouldn't end until the sun had set and the office was long empty.

But that was exactly how Simone had gotten to where she was. She'd climbed her way up from nothing, built her luxury hotel empire from the ground up, sacrificing everything for her career. Family. A social life. Romantic relationships. That was a price she was willing to pay. Love was nothing more than a fairy tale. Relationships always failed. She knew that all too well.

But she was only human. She had needs, just like any other woman. The difference was the kind of intimacy she craved.

And that was why she'd invested her precious time and energy into her new side venture. Club Velvet, a place for women to indulge in all of their deepest, wildest desires. She couldn't take all the credit for it. She was only one of several owners, and they'd all had a hand in bringing it to life. But Simone believed in Club Velvet as much as she believed in her hotel empire.

And she had no doubt that her investment would pay off. It had only been two days since the club opened, but the launch night party had been a success. Aside from one or two minor incidents.

Simone leaned back in her chair and stretched out her legs. There had been one particular incident, one encounter that had been playing in her mind ever since. Club Velvet had zero tolerance for harassment. That fact was expressly stated in the agreements the guests had to sign just to get in the door. And Simone had already made sure that the woman who called herself "Mistress T" was blacklisted from Club Velvet and all other clubs like it.

But she wasn't the person who was occupying Simone's thoughts. No, it was the young woman she'd preyed upon. That woman had occupied Simone's mind, danced through her thoughts, ever since. Her long, dark hair, which had flowed down her back like a curtain of silk. Those exquisite lips, the same pink as the blush on her cheeks. That little black dress, which clung to her voluptuous curves in the most enticing way—

Simone's office phone rang. She picked it up. It was the receptionist.

"Your 3 o'clock is here, Ms. Weiss. Should I send her in?"

My 3 o'clock? Simone brought up her calendar on the monitor in front of her. *3 p.m. Temp assistant final interview.*

"Of course," she said. "Send her through."

Simone hung up her phone. She'd forgotten all about the interview. Her assistant usually kept track of her meetings and appointments for her, but she was on maternity leave for the next three months.

Simone needed someone to fill in for her. And her ever industrious assistant had conducted the preliminary interviews for her replacement herself, hand picking the best possible candidate. All Simone had to do was conduct a final interview to confirm her assistant's choice.

Simone opened the candidate's file on her laptop. *Jade Fisher. Twenty-four years old.* Fresh out of the same MBA program Simone had plucked her regular assistant from. When it came to her employees, experience wasn't a priority for Simone. She preferred fast learners who were talented and committed, which often meant recent graduates.

Jade. Wasn't that the name of the woman she'd met at Club Velvet on Saturday night? The woman who had lit a fire within her with just a glance from those shimmering blue eyes?

The woman who had practically been begging for a Mistress?

Simone pulled herself together. Now wasn't the time for those kinds of thoughts. It seemed fate was toying with her by sending her an assistant with the same name.

There was a knock on her office door, followed by the receptionist's voice. "Jade is here."

"Come in," Simone called.

As the door to her office opened, she continued to scan Jade's file, committing the details to memory.

"Take a seat," Simone said. "I'll be with you in a moment."

But several seconds passed, and there was no movement in the room, no sound of footsteps on the marble floors. There was only silence.

Simone looked up from her laptop. Standing frozen in the doorway, a folder clutched to her chest, was a curvaceous young woman dressed in a light blue blouse, the same color as her eyes, and gray slacks and flats. Her long, dark hair was pulled back in a ponytail, her eyes wide with the same shock that was coursing through Simone's body.

The woman she met at Club Velvet that night? The woman her assistant had chosen as her replacement?

She was one and the same.

And she was standing in Simone's doorway.

CHAPTER 4

Jade's heart stopped. *It's her. It's really her.*

She stared at the woman sitting behind the desk, the very same woman who had rescued her at Club Velvet the other night. The woman who had offered to show her the private rooms, and more.

The woman who had haunted Jade's thoughts and filled her with desire and regret ever since.

Here she was again. Instead of a curve-hugging black dress, she wore a stylish ivory blazer and a dark pencil skirt, heels that were a more practical height. Her ice-blonde hair was pulled back into a tight bun, her lips a subtler shade of red.

But the way she looked at Jade, with intense curiosity mixed with desire? It was the same.

Simone cleared her throat. "I believe I told you to take a seat."

Jade blinked. "Yes."

"I don't like to repeat myself. Sit."

Regaining control of her body, Jade took a seat in one of

the chairs in front of Simone's desk. But she could barely look the woman in the eye.

How had she not noticed that the woman she'd spoken to that night was *Simone Weiss*? Jade had seen pictures of her before, online and in articles. Los Angeles' hotel queen was no stranger to the press. And Jade had researched her thoroughly in preparation for the interview.

But the woman Jade had met at Club Velvet was nothing like the severe executive from all those photos. And she never expected Los Angeles' wealthiest, most successful businesswoman to be mingling with the crowd that night. Not to mention, it had been dark, and Jade had been distracted by parts of the woman's body that weren't her face. The commanding seductress from Saturday night had seemed like someone else entirely.

Not that Simone was any less commanding as she sat behind her vast desk in her enormous corner office. And while her outfit wasn't as revealing as the dress she'd worn that night, the way her skirt hugged her hips and showed off her long legs was just as alluring.

Jade shook her head. "I'm sorry. I wasn't expecting this."

"Expecting what?" Simone asked. "Is there a problem?"

Jade opened her mouth to speak, then shut it again. So Simone wanted to pretend that Saturday night hadn't happened? Jade could work with that.

"No," she said. "There's no problem."

"Then let's begin." Simone shut her laptop and pushed it aside. "Since my assistant has already vetted you, I'll make this quick. She says you're the best candidate for the job. And I can't deny that for a recent graduate, your resume is impressive. You interned at Davis and Spencer?"

"Yes, I worked closely with the team responsible for—"

Simone held up her hand. "You don't need to sell me on your achievements. Your letter of recommendation tells me all I need to know. It's not every day that Carter Davis himself writes a personal recommendation for an intern. And your grad school professors gave glowing recommendations. I see you graduated at the top of your class, but you took an extra semester to complete the program. Why?"

Jade had hoped that wouldn't come up. "I took a semester off for personal reasons."

That was as much as she was willing to tell her future boss, or anyone else. Would Simone assume the worst? That Jade had burned out because she couldn't handle the stress of the rigorous MBA program?

That wasn't what had happened. But the truth about that period of her life was something she'd never told a single soul.

"I assume these personal issues have been resolved?" Simone asked.

"Yes," Jade said.

"And I assume you have no problem working in a high-pressure environment?"

"Of course. I thrive under pressure." She always had. It was how she'd made it through grad school, despite everything else that had been going on in her life.

"I hope that's true, because I need someone I can rely on now more than ever," Simone said. "I'm currently working on an important deal, an acquisition that *cannot* fail. And you'll be my right-hand woman on it. There will be long days, overtime, even the occasional weekend. Your compensation will reflect this, of course."

"That's not a problem. You can count on me."

Simone folded her hands on her desk. "Understand this,

Jade. I have the same expectations of my assistant as I have of myself. I expect you to work just as hard as me. I expect your work to be as close to perfection as humanly possible. And if you can't handle that, you'll be wasting not only your time, but mine."

Jade nodded. This was the Simone Weiss she'd heard about, the woman who had fought her way to the top through sheer force of will and a take-no-prisoners attitude. The woman in the club on Saturday night? While she'd been confident, commanding, she hadn't been so stern. And the icy look in Simone's eyes was enough to send shivers through her.

I'll show you the exquisite pleasures submission can bring...

Desire swelled inside Jade's body. She pushed it back down again. Would it be a mistake to take a job working for a woman who made her crumble with nothing more than a look?

But she needed the money, and the experience. While the position was only temporary, it was a stepping stone to something bigger. Executive assistant for Simone Weiss, CEO of the biggest hotel empire on the West Coast, the whole country, even? A recommendation from her would be worth a hundred times its weight in gold.

Jade needed this job.

Simone leaned forward, studying her intently. "Here's the deal. My assistant chose you out of dozens of candidates. She's been with me for years, and I trust her judgment. If she says you're the right person for the job, you're the right person for the job."

Jade held her breath, waiting for the inevitable *but*.

"But if you're going to be my assistant, we need to address the elephant in the room. Yes, we had... an encounter on Saturday night. But nothing came of it. So as far as I'm concerned, there's no conflict of interest. I'm willing to put what happened aside if you are."

Jade nodded. "I am."

"And you have a car?"

"Yes." It was falling apart, and long overdue for servicing, but it was better than nothing. A car was a necessity in LA.

"Good. I need my assistant to have a reliable mode of transport."

"Are you saying…"

"That the job is yours? Yes. I expect you here tomorrow at 8 a.m. And I don't tolerate lateness."

Jade nodded. "Yes, of course. Uh, thank you. For the opportunity." She cursed silently. She hadn't even started the job and she was already struggling to hold herself together.

Simone rose from her seat. "Now, if you'll excuse me, I have another appointment." She led Jade to the door and opened it up. "I'll see you tomorrow, 8 a.m. sharp."

"I'll be there," Jade said. "And thank you for taking a chance with me, despite, well, everything."

"Just don't make me regret it. Do not disappoint me."

Jade nodded. "I won't let you down."

She left Simone's office, her heart pounding. As she rode the elevator down to the ground floor, Simone's words echoed in her ears.

But in her mind's eye, it wasn't Simone Weiss speaking those words. Instead, it was the woman from Saturday night, clad in that black dress, standing barely an inch from her, scarlet lips whispering in her ear.

Do not disappoint me.

CHAPTER 5

"Good morning, Ms. Sloane," Jade said, her phone balanced on her shoulder as she opened Simone's inbox on her laptop. "I'm calling on behalf of Simone Weiss regarding your inquiry about featuring her in your magazine."

Jade searched through Simone's emails, keeping one ear on the phone conversation as she scrolled. *There.* The original blueprints for The Ashton Star. Jade had called and emailed a dozen different people to get her hands on a copy, all at Simone's request.

Jade forwarded the blueprints to the printer. She could pick them up after lunch.

"I believe she's available next Thursday afternoon," Jade said, bringing Simone's calendar up on the screen. "Does 3 p.m. work?"

She glanced at the time. It was ten minutes before she was due to leave to meet Renee for lunch. Simone was just as strict about enforcing lunch breaks as she was about everything else. Of course, it wasn't out of kindness.

Simone's reasoning was that regular breaks increased productivity. But Jade wasn't complaining. Her lunch breaks were her only respite from her long days.

"Wonderful. I'll let her know." She added the meeting to Simone's calendar. "Yes, I'll be sure to pass on the message."

She hung up the phone and took a sip of her coffee. The cup was almost empty. She needed to pace herself better. After all, it was only her first week.

And it had been a hectic week at that. Simone had made no attempt to ease her into her new role. Instead, she'd thrown Jade into the deep end, expecting her to handle everything from day one. Managing Simone's busy schedule. Screening her calls. Taking minutes at meetings. Even picking up her dry cleaning.

It was every bit as grueling as Simone had warned her. But with the help of the detailed instructions Simone's usual assistant had left her, Jade had risen to the challenge. Sure, it meant she'd stayed back late at the office every day of the week. Sure, she barely had time to do anything but work, eat, and sleep. But Jade liked being busy. It meant she didn't have time to think about anything else.

She switched back to Simone's inbox. She had enough time to reply to a few more emails before leaving for lunch. Or she could steal a couple of minutes to call her landlord about fixing the leak in the ceiling of her studio. She'd been trying to get a hold of him all week, but her voicemails and messages had gone unanswered.

Her laptop dinged, a memo popping up at the bottom corner of her screen. It was from Simone.

Come see me in my office.

She glanced at Simone's office door, which was a few

feet from Jade's desk. Why did she feel like she was being called into the principal's office?

Maybe because, in the four days since Jade had started working for her, all her hard work had gone unacknowledged. She hadn't gotten a single word of encouragement or praise from her new boss. But Simone had made it clear that she expected perfection. Why would she praise Jade for delivering what she'd asked for?

Jade sighed. She didn't need validation, not in her work life or her personal life. Yet a part of her craved just that from Simone for reasons she didn't understand.

Or maybe it wasn't her boss's praise she wanted. Maybe it was the praise of the woman she'd met at Club Velvet. That woman was right there in Simone's office, right there within Simone herself, just underneath the surface, waiting to come out...

Jade shook her head. Simone was her boss. They'd agreed to put Saturday night behind them, to keep things strictly professional. And Jade couldn't afford to risk her job with wild fantasies about her boss.

She got up from her desk and made her way to Simone's office, knocking on her door and announcing herself.

"Come in and take a seat," Simone said.

Jade opened the door. Inside, Simone sat behind her desk, her eyes fixed on her screen. Her lips were pursed in concentration, but Jade was still mesmerized by them, by her. She wore a sleeveless white dress that caressed every curve and dip of her body like she'd been sewn into it. And the heels adorning her feet?

They were the same shade of crimson as the heels she'd worn to Club Velvet that night.

Heat sparked deep in Jade's body. She'd been trying her

hardest not to think about that night, about how close she'd come to letting Simone show her a world of sensual pleasures she barely knew existed. But whenever she was in Simone's presence, all those thoughts came flooding back.

"Are you going to come in?" Simone said. "I don't have all day."

"Right. Yes." Jade shut the door and approached Simone's desk, taking a seat in front of it.

But despite Simone's comment, she took her time, typing away at her keyboard for a few more seconds. Then she turned her attention to Jade, looking her up and down.

Finally, she took a piece of paper from the side of her desk and slid it across the table. "What's this?"

Jade leaned forward, peering down at the page. "It's that memo you asked me to write for you."

"Do you see anything wrong with it?"

Jade scanned the memo through narrowed eyes. "I can't see anything." She looked up at Simone. "Did I make a mistake?"

Instead of answering her, Simone got up from her chair, rounded the desk, and leaned back against it, her fingers curling around the edge of the desktop. Jade's heart began to race. Simone was just inches from her, and Jade could feel the heat radiating from her. And her body, her bare legs, her luscious curves, were right in Jade's eyeline. She looked up at her boss's face, but Simone's unwavering gaze only made Jade hotter.

"When you started here, you were provided with everything you need to produce work to the standard I expect," Simone said. "You were given specific instructions for everything, from how I take my coffee to how to format documents, correct?"

Jade nodded.

"So why does this memo have my old letterhead on it?"

Jade blinked. "I must have missed that. It was only going out within the office, so I didn't think to check—"

"Know this," Simone interrupted. "When you're working for me, you need to be meticulous about all things at all times, even when it doesn't matter. It needs to become second nature, so that when the time comes that it *does* matter, you won't miss a thing. You won't make a single mistake. Because when you're working at my level, you *cannot* afford mistakes, understand?"

Jade nodded.

"Don't just nod. Tell me you understand what I'm saying to you."

"Yes. I understand."

"Look at me," Simone said firmly.

Jade obeyed.

"Everyone else in this office? I hold them to a high standard. But the reality is, if they slip up now and then, it won't do any harm."

She crossed her arms, framing her breasts. It was taking all of Jade's willpower not to drop her gaze. Could her boss see the flush on her cheeks?

"You, on the other hand?" Simone continued. "You are my assistant. You are an extension of me. From you, I expect *perfection*. And I wouldn't have hired you if I didn't think you were capable of it." She leaned down toward Jade. "Tell me I didn't make a mistake."

"You… you didn't."

"That's right. I don't make mistakes. I already know that. But I need you to know that, too."

"I understand," Jade said, her voice barely a whisper.

Simone's piercing amber eyes were still locked with hers. And she was so close, just as close as they'd been in the club that night…

"Then we're on the same page." Simone stood up. "You can go to lunch now."

Jade got to her feet and headed for the door, her legs shaking. *Pull yourself together.* But no amount of pleading would make her body listen to her.

"And Jade?"

She stopped at the door, turning back to her boss. "Yes?"

Simone rounded her desk and slid back into her chair, then crossed one leg over the other, her red heels flashing underneath her desk. "You've done an excellent job this week. I expect that to continue."

Jade nodded. "It will."

"Good girl."

Jade's whole body began to burn. She left the room, shutting the door behind her and taking a deep, steadying breath.

And as she gathered her things to go to lunch, Simone's parting words rang out in her ears.

CHAPTER 6

J ade slipped into the seat across from Renee. "Sorry I'm late. My boss called me into her office at the last minute."

"No worries." Renee pushed an oversized iced coffee and a BLT across the table. "I got your usual."

Jade murmured a thanks and took a swig of her coffee, then started on the sandwich. She and Renee had been having lunch together every few weeks at the same cafe downtown for years. Luckily, it was just a few minutes from Jade's new job.

"I hope you weren't in trouble with the boss," Renee said.

Jade grimaced. "It was nothing. I used the wrong letterhead on a memo and got a lecture about it."

Renee raised an eyebrow. "You weren't kidding about this woman being strict."

"Oh, she's strict, all right."

Strict. Disciplined. Oh so commanding. And every time Simone gave Jade an order, she'd go weak at the knees, her mind filling with thoughts of Simone ordering her to do entirely unprofessional things. And what Simone had said to her before she left for lunch had only made those thoughts worse.

Good girl. Had Simone really said those words? Had Jade imagined it?

Why had it made her feel hot all over?

"I don't get it," Renee said. "If she's such an asshole, why do you want to work for her so badly?"

Jade swallowed her mouthful of sandwich. "She's not an asshole. She has high expectations, that's all. And that's how she became one of the most successful businesswomen in the country in the first place. That's why I wanted to work for her. I'm getting a real behind-the-scenes look at what it's like to run a company like hers. And that kind of experience is priceless."

After all, Jade didn't want to be an assistant forever. She had bigger goals. She was going to climb the ladder, just like Simone had. And one day, she would start her own company, just like Simone.

But she had to start from the bottom. And working for Simone, learning from the very best, was the perfect first step. While the job was only temporary, it would give Jade the foundation she needed to build a career of her own.

"Well, I hope it's worth it," Renee said.

"So do I. Because honestly, I'm starting to wonder if working for her was a mistake. Not because she's so strict, but because, well…"

Jade hesitated. She hadn't told Renee about Simone and the woman from Club Velvet being the same person. She'd been so busy with her new job that they'd barely spoken at all.

"Because what?" Renee asked. "What aren't you telling me?"

"It's a little crazy." Jade took a long, slow sip of her coffee. "You know that woman I was talking to at Club Velvet the other night?"

"You mean the hot blonde Amazon?"

"Yeah, her. You're not going to believe this, but that was Simone. Simone Weiss."

Renee's eyes widened. "You mean your new *boss*?"

Jade nodded. "I didn't realize it was her until the interview."

"You're kidding. What are the chances of that?"

"I don't know, but I don't exactly feel lucky. I'm stuck spending ten hours a day with this woman who gets me all hot and flustered just by looking at me."

Renee smirked. "So she's your type, huh? I figured as much. Especially after watching you drool over all the Dommes at Club Velvet."

"It's not like that, Ree. And I wasn't drooling over anyone. I'm not into that kind of thing. And even if I was, my boss would be the last person I'd want to do that with."

"Uh-huh. Then why are you blushing right now?"

Jade folded her arms across her chest. She didn't have a retort for that. Because Renee was right. Jade *was* into that kind of thing. Or at the very least, she was curious. She had been ever since Simone had offered to show her the ropes at Club Velvet.

For a moment, a tantalizing image of Simone binding her up in ropes, leaving her powerless, helpless, flashed behind her eyes. And with it came Simone's words from just minutes ago, echoing through her mind, reverberating through her body, all the way down to her core—

"Hello?" Renee said. "Are you even listening to me?"

Jade nodded. "Sorry, I'm all over the place right now. And not just because of Simone."

"Is everything okay?"

"I've just got my hands full at the moment. This new job is really intense, which I can handle, but it's an adjustment. And it doesn't leave me with much time to deal with everything else that's going on right now. Like my car. It's making weird noises, but I can't afford to take it to a mechanic until I get my first paycheck. But that's earmarked for all the other bills that are already piling up. Oh, and I've spent the entire week trying to get my landlord to fix this leak in the ceiling of my studio, but he's ignoring my calls. And I haven't had a chance to chase him up because it's like I'm working every day from the moment I wake up to the moment I go to sleep!"

"Wow," Renee said. "That's a lot."

"You're telling me." Jade pushed her half-eaten sandwich away. "But it's nothing I can't handle."

Renee shook her head. "I don't know how you do it. You know, keep it together all the time. When the rest of us were panicking during finals, you were fine."

"Maybe that's because I actually studied instead of going to parties all the time."

"Hey, I passed all my classes, didn't I? Maybe I wasn't valedictorian like you, but we aren't all blessed with your brains and cool head."

"You make it sound like it was easy for me. Maybe it looked that way from the outside, but I worked hard for all of that."

And not just in college. Jade had worked her entire life to get to where she was. She'd been the first person in her family to go to college, and on a full-ride scholarship at that. It was all so she could escape her tiny, one-stoplight home-town and build the life she wanted for herself.

Sure, she'd had missteps along the way, especially during grad school. She'd let herself get distracted, let her guard down, trusted someone she shouldn't have. Her heart had been crushed, her whole life shattered, and she hadn't been able to tell a single soul.

She'd picked herself back up in the end. But the scars remained.

"Well, just make sure you're not working too hard," Renee said. "Pushing yourself all the time is a surefire way to burn out."

It wasn't hard to figure out what Renee meant. *You don't want to burn out like you did in grad school.* But that hadn't had anything to do with burnout. Jade had let Renee and everyone else believe that because it was easier than telling them the truth.

"I'll be fine. This is nothing I haven't dealt with before." Jade picked at her sandwich absently. "Well, except for everything with Simone. I have no idea what to do about that."

Renee chuckled. "*That's* the one thing you don't know how to handle? Being around a woman you're into?"

"It's more than that. More than just attraction. When-ever I'm around her, I just can't stop my heart from racing. And whenever I'm not around her, I can't stop thinking about her." Jade put her head in her hands. "I've never felt like this before. What am I supposed to do?"

"The only thing you can do. Keep your head down, get your job done, and buy plenty of batteries."

"Batteries? Why would I need—" Heat crept up Jade's face. "Seriously?"

Renee shrugged. "It'll scratch that Simone itch *and* relieve stress. Kill two birds with one vibe."

Jade shook her head. "You're ridiculous."

The conversation moved on. And before Jade knew it, she had only five minutes left of her lunch break.

"I should get going," she said. "I can't be late in getting back."

"Right," Renee said. "You wouldn't want to get on the boss's bad side. Especially since you know how she'd punish you."

"That's *not* funny."

But that didn't stop a scene from forming in Jade's mind. Of her returning to the office a few minutes late. Of Simone giving her a lecture before enacting some kind of kinky punishment. Tying Jade to that imposing leather desk chair of hers. Making Jade kneel at her feet. Bending her over her desk and spanking her…

Jade banished the image from her mind. When had her imagination become so dirty?

She wrapped up the rest of her sandwich and stashed it in her purse for later. "Let's get out of here."

They left the cafe, parting ways at the door. As Jade began the short walk back to her office, she pulled out her phone and dialed her landlord's number. But like the last three times she called, it went straight to voicemail.

Great. Another night of listening to water dripping into a bucket. She needed to find a better apartment. One with a roof that didn't leak and appliances that worked. Maybe even something with more than one room.

She left another message and hung up, pushing the problem to the back of her mind, along with everything else. Despite what she'd told Renee, she was starting to feel the pressure of it all. Her apartment. Her money troubles. The long work hours.

The fact that she was stuck spending her days with a woman she found irresistible, despite how coldly she treated her.

Simone's words echoed in her mind. *Good girl.* That wasn't the kind of thing any boss would say to an employee, let alone one as impassive as Simone. But she'd said it. Jade hadn't imagined it.

So why had Simone spoken those words to her?

CHAPTER 7

S imone stared at her monitor, her phone on speaker on the desk beside her keyboard. "And why are you sending me photos of half-naked women while I'm in the office?"

"When else am I going to send them to you?" Elle said, her voice echoing through the phone. "You're always in the office."

"I have a company to run."

"So do I. Why do you think I'm at Club Velvet tonight? Someone has to keep an eye on our little venture."

"I'm sure that's why you're there tonight," Simone murmured. Along with being one of the other owners of Club Velvet, Elle ran her own company, which owned dozens of bars and nightclubs across the city. While she played an important role in creating and managing Club Velvet, she tended to get distracted by every pretty woman who crossed her path.

"I'm going to pretend I didn't hear that," Elle said. "Tell me what you think of the photos. They're the work of the rope artist I was telling you about. I sent you a link to her website."

Simone clicked the link. The website was filled with yet more images of women in various states of undress, artfully bound with ropes.

"I already spoke to her," Elle said. "Told her we were looking for a shibari artist for performances and hands-on demonstrations, maybe even some classes. She was very into the idea."

"She's certainly talented," Simone said. "Let's hire her for a performance in The Playroom next Saturday night. If it goes well, we can discuss a regular arrangement."

There was a knock on Simone's office door. It had to be Jade. She and Simone were the only people left in the office this late at night.

"One moment," she called before speaking more quietly to Elle. "I need to go. Let's talk later."

She hung up the phone and closed the website. She didn't need Jade hearing or seeing anything to do with club business. It was entirely inappropriate for her assistant to know about her tastes. It was bad enough that Jade had seen her at Club Velvet.

But Jade had been at the club that night too. And she'd admitted to Simone that she was curious. Not that she'd needed to say so. Her curiosity had been clear on her face. So had her interest in Simone.

But Jade had turned her down. Which had been the right move, in the end. If anything had happened between them that night, hiring her would have been a conflict of interest.

Yes, it was for the best. After all, there were very few people who met Simone's requirements for an assistant.

Women who were eager to play, on the other hand? They were plentiful.

But none of them were Jade. None of them were so utterly alluring.

None of them lit a fire inside her like Jade did.

Simone pushed the thought aside. "Come in."

Jade opened the door and approached Simone's desk tentatively. Things between them had been tense since day one. Simone's little slip-up the week before hadn't helped.

Good girl. She hadn't meant to say those words to Jade. It was entirely unprofessional.

But at that moment, Jade hadn't been her assistant. She'd been an eager-to-please woman who had spent the whole week serving every one of Simone's needs with the devotion of a submissive to her Mistress. And so, Simone had slipped into a dynamic that was just as natural to her as boss and employee.

It had been a mistake. A lapse. But Simone hadn't missed the way her assistant had reacted.

Jade had *liked* it.

Simone looked up at her. "Yes, Jade?"

"You got an email," she said. "I thought it was important enough that you'd want to hear the news right away. It's about The Ashton Star. There's another party interested in it."

Simone opened her emails. There it was, in black and white. Orion Development was eyeing her hotel. And they wanted to knock it down and build a parking lot, of all things.

She held back a curse. Until now, she'd been the only party interested in buying The Ashton Star. At least, the

47

only party with enough money to stand a chance. Now, she had competition.

"My assistant put together a file on Orion Development earlier in the year," Simone said. "Find it and send it to me. I need you to read it too. I want you on top of everything to do with Orion."

Jade nodded. "Right away."

She left the room hurriedly. She seemed even more flustered than usual. Simone didn't need that right now. She needed her assistant at the top of her game, especially with the roadblock that had been dropped in her path.

Simone leaned back in her chair and stretched out. She'd had her eye on The Ashton Star for years. The old hotel had been the jewel of the city once, but now the cracks were beginning to show. The building was in dire need of restoration, and it was becoming more and more costly to keep it running. But the owners, the Ashton family, had steadfastly refused to sell it.

Until now.

Simone had to get her hands on it, no matter what it took. Hotels in Los Angeles were a dime a dozen. Luxury hotels were rarer, but still plentiful. The Ashton Star? It was a step above them all. It was a Los Angeles landmark, known all over the world. A shining star in the heart of the city.

But it was more than that to Simone. It was *her* star, representing everything that she'd spent her career striving for. Her career was everything to her. The success, the independence it brought her, were everything.

Make sure you can stand on your own two feet, no matter what. Make sure no one can take away what you've got. Then you'll never have to rely on any man. That was what her mother had told her so many times before. And while there had never been a chance of Simone ending up with a man, she'd taken her mother's words to heart. After her father left them, she'd watched her mother struggle to put food on the table and keep a roof over their heads. And she'd vowed her life would be different.

Simone had kept that promise to her young self. She'd become successful enough that she'd never need to rely on anyone else. And she'd poured everything she had into her company to achieve that.

Which was why acquiring The Ashton Star was so important. She would restore it to its former glory, transform it into something grand. The crown jewel of her hotel empire, her most treasured prize.

Simone was so close to making it hers. She'd had countless meetings with the Ashtons' lawyers, their executives, all building up to meeting with the one person who mattered—Marissa Ashton herself. She was the head of the family, the company. She was who Simone needed to persuade to sell her the hotel.

And sooner rather than later. Simone had entertained the endless back and forth, biding her time, because that was how the game was played. But now that there was another player on the board, she needed to act fast.

She refreshed her emails. Jade hadn't sent her the file yet. It shouldn't have taken more than a minute.

Simone got up from her chair and opened her office door. Her assistant's desk was only a few feet from it. Jade sat there, her phone to her ear, murmuring into it. And when she hung up, she didn't notice Simone's presence. She just put the phone down on her desk, staring blankly ahead.

Simone cleared her throat. "The Orion file, Jade?"

Jade jumped in her seat. "Right. One second."

Simone crossed her arms, watching as Jade fiddled with her laptop, her brows drawn together in concentration. Seconds passed in silence. And as the silence stretched out, Jade's expression shifted from focused to concerned.

"Is something the matter?" Simone asked.

"It's…" Jade blinked. "It's gone. The file is gone."

"What do you mean? *Where* has it gone?"

"I don't know. I tried to open it and…" Jade shook her head. "I don't know what happened. I must have deleted it by accident. It's just not here anymore."

Simone let out a heavy sigh. "Look, it's been a long day. Just go home. It's too late to call IT about fixing this mess you've made, so do it first thing in the morning."

But instead of nodding dutifully like usual, Jade's lip began to quiver.

"I'm sorry." Her voice shook, as if she were on the verge of tears. "I'm really sorry."

"It's just a file," Simone said. "IT can restore it."

But Jade barely seemed to hear her. "I don't know how this happened. I don't know what I did. Everything is going wrong."

She hugged her arms to her chest as if to hold herself together. But her whole body trembled, her eyes glistening with tears. She was moments from falling apart.

And for the second time since Jade started working for her, Simone slipped into a dynamic that was entirely unprofessional.

"Stand up," she said firmly.

Jade glanced up at her, hesitation in her eyes.

"I already told you, I don't like to repeat myself." Simone crossed her arms. "*Stand. Up.*"

Jade got to her feet, her eyes downcast.

"Look at me."

Jade obeyed.

"Listen. The file isn't gone. The servers back up everything regularly. IT can restore it, understand?"

Jaded nodded.

"Now, I know a missing file isn't enough to throw you like this," Simone said. "So I need you to tell me what's really going on. If you can't handle the work I'm giving you—"

"It's not that," Jade said. "This isn't about work. I can do my job, I swear."

"Then tell me what's wrong."

"I've just got a lot going on right now. And I just got a phone call that—" Jade's voice cracked, her body trembling again.

Simone put her hands on Jade's shoulders, looking deep into her eyes. "Take a deep breath for me. Then another. Keep breathing, just like that." She waited for Jade to calm down. "Now, you said you got a phone call?"

Jade nodded. "I got a call, and…" She swallowed. "It was my landlord. A pipe burst in my apartment. Everything is flooded. I can't go back there tonight. Or maybe ever. I have nowhere to go. And my things… What if they're ruined?" She drew in a deep breath, steadying herself. "I'm sorry. This isn't your problem."

"Of course it's my problem. You're my assistant. You're no use to me like this. I'm not going to leave you with nowhere to go."

"I'll figure out something. I can find a room somewhere. Or stay on a friend's couch."

"I won't have you sleeping on a couch or running around

trying to find a hotel room at this time of night. No, you're coming with me. And the first thing we're going to do is get you something to eat because you haven't had anything since lunch, have you?"

"I guess I forgot," Jade said. "I've been so busy."

"I'll order dinner for us now. That way, it will have arrived by the time we get home."

Jade blinked. "Home?"

"Yes, you'll stay with me tonight."

"You want me to come home with you?"

As soon as the words left Jade's mouth, her cheeks turned pink.

"You'll sleep in the guest room, of course," Simone said.

"Of course. But I..." Jade shook her head. "I appreciate the offer, really, but I can't accept all this. I'll f—"

"Figure something out? Jade, it's late. You're stressed. You're exhausted. *Let me help you.*" Simone ran her hand down Jade's arm. "Let me take care of this for you."

Jade looked up at her. And for a moment, her eyes shimmered, not with tears, but with longing, desire. And they stirred the same in Simone, the lust she'd buried deep the first day Jade had walked into her office. Could Jade see it in her, feel it?

Could she hear all that went unspoken in Simone's words?

"I'll..." Jade's voice was barely a whisper. "I'll come with you."

CHAPTER 8

J ade was woken up the next morning by the kiss of the morning sun on her face.

Sunlight? Hardly any sun reached her studio, morning or otherwise. She groaned and opened her eyes, squinting at her surroundings. Sunlight. Bright white curtains. A soft bed she could stretch her arms across and not touch the ends of.

Jade wasn't in her studio. She wasn't in her bed. She was in Simone's Beverly Hills mansion.

She buried her head in the pillow. How had she ended up here, in the guest room of the woman she'd spent almost two weeks trying desperately to ignore her attraction to? The previous night was a complete blur. She'd gotten the phone call from her landlord. She'd lost the file. She'd almost burst into tears in front of her boss.

But Simone had taken control, snapping her out of hysterics and insisting on taking care of everything.

What happened next felt like a dream. Simone had brought her back to her home, sat there while Jade finished off her dinner. She'd run Jade a bath in the jacuzzi in her ensuite before making up the guest bedroom with fresh linens, laying out a pair of soft cotton pajamas and a fluffy dressing gown for Jade to wear. And she'd sent Jade to bed, a glass of water on her nightstand, leaving the light in the hall on for her.

And Jade, exhausted and distraught, had acquiesced to it all without a single word. She'd passed out the moment her head hit the pillow. And now, the morning after?

She felt incredible.

She rolled onto her back, stretching out her body. She couldn't remember the last time she'd felt so refreshed. It was as if she was lighter, unburdened of all her problems. Her rattling car, her flooded apartment, her job—it all felt miles away.

And all because of Simone.

Her stomach fluttered. She'd never had anyone take care of her like that before. Had the same woman who hardly said a word to her beyond giving orders, who lectured her for the simplest of mistakes, really done everything short of tucking Jade into bed last night?

But maybe it hadn't been Simone, her boss. Maybe it had been the woman Jade met at Club Velvet, who had come to her rescue, seduced her with the promise of sensual delights that made Jade's whole body burn...

Jade sat upright, her heart thumping hard. She needed to get out of here. She shouldn't have let Simone take her home in the first place. She shouldn't have let those lines blur, just like she had years ago...

She took a deep breath. *Just stay calm.* She glanced at the clock on the nightstand. It was still early, but knowing

Simone's schedule, she'd be awake already. Could Jade sneak out of her house without her noticing?

She got out of bed and grabbed her phone from the nightstand, where it had been plugged into a charger. She had no memory of doing that herself, so that must have been Simone too. Spotting her purse on the dressing table nearby, Jade slid her phone into it, gathered her clothes from the day before, and got dressed.

Once she was finished, she attempted to fix her hair in the mirror, pulling it out of the loose ponytail she'd slept with it in and running her fingers through it. Without a hairbrush, trying to tie it up again was pointless, so she gathered it over one shoulder, grabbed her things, and slipped out of the room.

Shutting the door as quietly as she could, she glanced down the hall. There was no sign of Simone. The coast was clear.

She made her way to the stairs barefoot, her flats held in her hand, taking care not to make a sound on the hardwood floors. But as she reached the bottom of the stairs, a familiar scent reached her.

Pancakes? Is Simone making pancakes?

Jade glanced at the front door. It was only a few steps away. If she moved quickly, she could still make it out undetected—

"Good, you're awake."

Jade turned toward the kitchen. Simone stood in the wide doorway, dressed in a long silk robe. It was belted at the waist, enhancing her every curve, a long leg peeking out from under it. Her blonde hair was loose, flowing down her back and shoulders in waves.

She gestured toward the dining table. "Breakfast will be ready in a moment."

Jade glanced at the table, where two places were set. Her boss was making her breakfast?

"Don't just stand there," Simone said. "*Sit.*"

Jade hesitated. Then, abandoning her purse and shoes by the door, she sat down at the dining table.

"Now, how do you take your eggs?" Simone asked.

"Um, sunny side up," Jade said.

Simone nodded. "It'll be another few minutes. Make yourself comfortable."

As Simone disappeared into the kitchen, Jade gazed around the room, trying to make sense of her surroundings. She could hardly remember arriving the night before, and it had been dark.

But in the light of day, Simone's mansion was breathtaking. The vast, open living space had high ceilings and a grand fireplace, antique furniture filling the room. Floor-to-ceiling windows offered sweeping views of the hills, and the double doors nearby were flung open to reveal a deck surrounded by plants and trees. Beyond it was a crystal-clear infinity pool that seemed to stretch out into the horizon, merging with the blue sky above.

Jade was still taking it all in when Simone reappeared, a pot of coffee and two mugs in her hands. She set them down on the table, pouring them each a cup of coffee and adding milk to Jade's before returning to the kitchen. She emerged again a moment later, carrying two plates of pancakes, eggs, and bacon.

"Here." She placed them on the dining table, one in front of Jade. "Eat."

Jade stared at her plate. The food looked just as delicious

as it smelled. But she could hardly believe that Simone had cooked her breakfast in the first place.

Simone placed a hand on her hip, her robe parting slightly to reveal a flash of pale chest. "Is something the matter?"

"No," Jade said. "This looks amazing."

She picked up her knife and fork and took a small bite of her pancakes. That seemed to satisfy Simone, who sat down across from her and started on her own breakfast.

Jade took another bite, then another. She hadn't realized how hungry she was. She picked up her coffee and took a long gulp. Milk, no sugar. That was how she took it. But how had Simone known? Jade always got coffee for her, never the other way around.

Before she knew it, she'd cleaned her plate. But she barely had a chance to put her fork down before Simone offered her seconds.

Jade shook her head. "I'm good. Thank you. For breakfast, and for everything last night. But I..."

Simone cocked her head. "Yes?"

"I don't mean to sound ungrateful, but why are you doing all this for me?"

Simone set her coffee cup down on a coaster. "I'm doing this because you need it, Jade." She leaned forward, amber eyes fixed on Jade's. "You are my assistant. I need you at your best. But you've been working nonstop with no regard for your own well-being. So if you won't take care of yourself, I will, understand?"

Jade's cheeks grew hot. "I understand."

Simone sat back in her chair. "Now, you'll want to take the morning off to address the situation with your apartment. If you need more time, let me know. Otherwise, I expect you in the office this afternoon."

Jade nodded.

"You can freshen up and get dressed before you leave. I ordered you some things last night. They were delivered this morning. Clothes to wear, and so on."

Jade blinked. "You bought me clothes?"

"Among other things," Simone said. "Sundries, a phone charger. Since you can't get into your apartment, you'll need enough essentials to last the next few days at least."

"I don't know what to say. You didn't have to do that."

"Again, I did. I think we can both agree that you have enough on your plate right now as it is. You're no use to me if you're too swamped to do your job."

"I…" But there was no point protesting. "Thank you."

"Don't mention it," Simone said. "Now, go get ready. You can use the bathroom across the hall from the guest room. You'll find everything you need inside. I'll leave the things I got for you on the bed. Once you're dressed and ready, I'll have my driver take us back to the office so you can get your car."

Jade nodded and got up from the dining table, making her way upstairs and into the bathroom. After the most lavish bath of her life the night before, in Simone's ensuite no less, she didn't need to shower. But she did need to make herself more presentable.

As Simone had promised, she found everything she needed in the bathroom, from a hairbrush to a facewash and moisturizer set with the most heavenly scent and silky feel. After washing her face and brushing her teeth, she ran the hairbrush through her hair and pulled it up into a loose bun.

When she returned to the guest room, the bed had been made. On top of it was an empty leather duffel bag, a small bag of toiletries, and some carefully folded clothes. A pair of jeans, a sweater, some t-shirts, light canvas shoes, pajamas. Even socks and panties.

Jade's face began to burn. She picked up one of the pairs of panties. Like everything else on the bed, they were her exact size. They were the style Jade normally wore, too. How had Simone known? It was as impressive as it was mortifying.

But Jade was already flustered enough. Thinking about her boss buying her panties was *not* helping.

She examined the rest of the clothing on the bed, which was mostly workwear. A dress, a couple of skirts, some blouses, all in clear garment bags. Jade picked up one of the garment bags and opened it up. Inside was a royal blue blouse made of a silky, delicate fabric. No, not *silky*. It was real silk. And a glance at the tag told her it was designer.

She ran her hand over the fabric of the blouse. It was luxuriously soft. How much had it cost? Each of the items on the bed looked more expensive than anything Jade owned. And Simone had bought them for her without a second thought?

As she placed the blouse down, her eyes fell upon a dress laid out on the bed. Unlike the others, it wasn't in a garment bag. It had been set aside carefully, deliberately.

Almost as if Simone wanted her to wear it.

Jade's heart skipped. One thing was clear—Simone liked to take charge in the office *and* in the bedroom. Was she taking charge of Jade now, too? Exerting control over her for her own satisfaction?

Jade shook her head. That was a crazy thought.

So why did it send a thrill through her body?

She stripped off her clothes from the day before, picked up the dress, and slipped into it. The plum-colored sheath dress ended just above the knee, with a wide boat neck and a subtle diamond pattern to the fabric. It was nothing risqué. Nothing that would look out of place in the office. But when Jade looked at herself in the full-length mirror in the corner of the room?

Wow.

Where had Simone found a dress like this? Most of the clothes Jade could find in her size were shapeless and unflattering or looked like something her grandma would wear.

But this dress? It fit her body as if it were tailored for it, showing off her every curve, giving her the hourglass silhouette of a 50s pinup model. And while the dress wasn't at all revealing, the low, wide neck framed her shoulders and collarbones in an almost flirtatious way. She looked sexy. *Felt* sexy.

Would Simone feel the same when she saw Jade wearing the dress?

Would she want to tear it off?

Jade pulled herself together. She had far too much to do to waste time fantasizing. And she needed to get out of Simone's mansion before she lost her mind completely.

Packing everything Simone had bought her into the duffel bag, she left the room, returning downstairs to find Simone sitting in a leather armchair. She'd gotten dressed for work and was finishing off her coffee.

As Jade set the duffel bag next to her purse by the front door, Simone looked up at her, her gaze skimming over Jade's body and up to her eyes.

Jade's breath caught in her chest. There was a hunger in Simone's gaze, a satisfaction, a *desire*. Had Jade been right? Had Simone laid out the dress for her to wear for her own pleasure?

Simone rose to her feet, beckoning Jade with a finger. "Come here."

Jade's body obeyed before her mind did, moving to stand before her. Leaning in close, Simone reached up and took a stray strand of Jade's hair, brushing it behind her ear.

"Perfect," Simone whispered, tracing her thumb down Jade's cheek with a feather-light touch. "You're perfection."

Jade trembled, heat flaring inside her. Simone's ruby-red lips were only inches from Jade's own. And her eyes, they drew Jade even closer, their magnetic pull impossible to resist, until she could feel Simone's breath on her cheek—

Suddenly, Simone pulled her hand back, as if shocked by electricity.

Jade's stomach sank, the sting of rejection stabbing inside her chest. She took a step back, then another.

"I need to go," she stammered.

Simone didn't try to stop her. She didn't say a word. She only offered Jade a silent nod.

Her pulse thundering in her ears, Jade walked over to her bags and picked them up. And as she opened the front door and left the mansion, she didn't dare look back.

It wasn't until she was out on the street that she allowed herself to breathe. She looked around, cursing to herself. She'd lost her chance at getting a ride back to her car.

But spending what little money she had on a rideshare was better than spending another moment in Simone's presence. Because in that one brief moment Simone had touched her? That single moment when they'd stepped over the line they'd drawn, let the forbidden spark between them ignite? She'd nearly lost herself.

It excited her. And it scared her.

Because Jade had lost herself in someone else before. And it had almost cost her everything.

CHAPTER 9

Jade stepped into Simone's office, a bag of Chinese takeout in her hand. Simone sat behind her desk, a phone held to her ear.

Taking care not to disturb her, Jade set the bag of takeout on her desk and began unpacking it, her stomach rumbling. She hadn't eaten since lunch, and it was getting late.

"Send it to me as soon as you can," Simone said into the phone. "I'll take a look at it later."

Jade finished setting out the food and turned to leave. But as she did, Simone held up a finger.

"I need to go. We'll speak tomorrow." She hung up the phone, then pushed one of the takeout boxes and a pair of chopsticks across the desk toward Jade. "This is for you."

"Thanks," Jade said. "But you don't need to keep doing this." It was the third time Simone had bought her dinner that week.

"Of course I do. You're no use to me if you're halfway to

passing out. You need to make sure you're eating regular meals."

"That was only once," Jade murmured. She'd been distracted that evening, even before the phone call.

"Was it? Because that wasn't the first time I noticed you staying late without dinner."

Jade's cheeks burned. She had a bad habit of skipping meals when she was busy, but she didn't think Simone had noticed. "It won't happen again."

"No, it won't." Simone picked up a file from her desk and began flipping through it. "You may go. And let me know when you've finished with the building report."

Jade picked up the box of takeout and left Simone's office, taking a seat at her desk. Somehow, she'd survived another week of working for Simone. And it had been just as exhilarating as it had been excruciating.

Why had it been so exhilarating? Because, after almost three weeks as Simone's assistant, they worked together seamlessly. Jade anticipated every one of her boss's needs, from making sure her coffee cup was never empty to having her schedule memorized down to the minute. Simone was entrusting her with important tasks more and more. And Jade completed every one of them flawlessly, sometimes before Simone even asked her to, basking in every sliver of praise she offered her.

But that was what made it excruciating. All those little bits of praise? They only fueled Jade's desire to serve her boss's every whim and need. She was irrevocably drawn to Simone's dominant manner. And after that night at her mansion, Simone had become even more dominant, taking charge of Jade from the moment she stepped into the office to the moment she walked out the door.

If you won't take care of yourself, I will. Those had been Simone's words that night. And she was making good on her vow. Buying her assistant dinner every other night was just the tip of the iceberg. If Jade hadn't left for lunch by 1 p.m., Simone would insist that she take a break immediately. She'd bring Jade coffee—milk, no sugar—when she went to the coffee shop downstairs to stretch her legs every afternoon. And if Jade tried to stay later than her at work, Simone would send her home, not taking no for an answer.

And thanks to Simone, Jade now had a home to go to, at least temporarily. Her studio was still unusable, so her landlord had offered her another apartment to stay in, but it was on the outskirts of the city, more than an hour from the office in traffic. And when Jade had told her boss this, Simone had insisted that she stay in one of her hotels downtown instead, ignoring all of Jade's protests.

But she'd stopped protesting when she saw the hotel room. The five-star suite was far nicer than any apartment or hotel she'd ever stayed in. It even had a separate living room.

Jade opened the box of takeout and picked up her chopsticks, starting on her dinner. She hadn't missed the fact that when she'd tried to thank her boss for it, Simone had brushed her off, and with the same line as always.

You're no use to me if you're too swamped to do your job.

You're no use to me if you don't have a place to stay.

You're no use to me if you're dead on your feet.

From the very beginning, Simone had made it clear that she had high expectations of her assistant. She needed Jade at the top of her game. That was why she was helping her.

But was it the *only* reason why?

As Jade raised her chopsticks to her mouth, a clump of

rice fell onto her dress. She held back a curse, grabbing a tissue to wipe it up. She had only been able to retrieve a few essentials from her flooded apartment, so she was still relying on the outfits Simone had bought her. The dress she'd worn today, a dark gray A-line number with a matching belt, was one of her favorites. It looked just as enticing on her as the other dress had.

Had Simone noticed it, noticed Jade in it? She hadn't said anything, but the moment Jade walked into the office in it, Simone's gaze had flicked over her body hungrily, drinking her in, just like in Simone's mansion that morning.

Jade let out a deep sigh. She liked it when Simone looked at her that way. She liked it when Simone took charge, commanding her with that firm but velvet-smooth voice.

And she desperately wished for Simone to command her to do far more than fetch her coffee...

Focus, Jade. She wiped up the last of the mess on her dress and tossed the tissue in the bin. Picking up her chopsticks, she began flipping through the document in front of her. It was a building report for The Ashton Star, the hotel Simone was set on buying.

And somehow, Jade had become invested in the project, too. The Ashton Star was a beautiful old building. Knocking it down and replacing it with a parking lot seemed like such a waste. The idea of saving it, restoring it, was almost romantic.

Not that Jade was a romantic. She had been, once upon a time. It was why she'd left her hometown for Los Angeles. She'd had her pick of half a dozen colleges in half a dozen cities around the country.

But in the end, she'd chosen Los Angeles. Because she'd always dreamed of something more than her small-town life. And if there was anywhere she could find what she was searching for, it was in the city of dreams, where anything was possible.

Of course, after she'd moved here, she'd quickly realized that Los Angeles wasn't all it was cracked up to be. The city was nowhere near as glamorous as it appeared from the outside. But that hadn't been enough to kill the romantic in her. No, that had happened later.

But Jade didn't want to think about that now. She took another bite of her dinner and flipped to the next page of the building report. Simone had tasked her with reading it and flagging anything important. It was by far the most boring task Simone had ever given her. It was page after page of building codes and zoning regulations, descriptions of cracks in the brickwork, crumbling plaster, drainage defects...

Huh? Drainage defects?

Jade paused, her chopsticks halfway to her mouth as she read the paragraph again. *Does Simone know about this?* It seemed important. But it was buried on the 32nd page of the report.

She finished off the rest of her food. She had research to do.

Ten minutes later, she headed into her boss's office, the report in her hand. Simone had finished her dinner and was typing away at her computer, her eyes fixed on her monitor.

"Yes, Jade?" she murmured.

Jade stepped up to Simone's desk. "I think I found something in the building report."

Simone finally looked up at her. "Show me."

"Here, it's on page 32." Jade handed the report to her. "There's an issue with the drainage under the building. It was supposed to be fixed by the end of last year, but I couldn't find any records of that happening. I don't think it's been fixed at all."

Simone scanned the page with narrowed eyes. "You're right. Jade, you're right." She stood up, flipping to the next page. "This is huge. You know what this means, don't you?"

"Uh…"

But Simone didn't wait for her to answer. "Whoever buys the hotel will need to fix this, even if they're only going to knock the building down. It will cost a small fortune." She began pacing beside her desk. "Orion Development is looking for an easy investment. They won't want to fork out any extra money. This? This will kill their interest completely. They'll be out of the running."

"That's great," Jade said.

"I can't believe I missed this. I completely missed this." Simone stopped in front of her. "But *you* didn't."

"It was nothing," Jade said.

"No." Simone shook her head. "No, this was deliberately buried. For you to have spotted this, for you to know how important this is… Jade, you're a star. You're brilliant."

Simone stepped toward her, closing the distance that remained between them. And suddenly, Jade was frozen, Simone's gaze pinning her in place.

"You're *brilliant*," Simone said, her voice dropping to a whisper. "You're so brilliant I could just…"

It happened in the space of a heartbeat. But at the same time, the world around them seemed to slow and blur.

Simone reached out and cupped Jade's cheek in her hand, drawing her thumb along her lower lip.

Jade quivered, her lips parting obediently, a soft breath spilling from them.

She closed her eyes.

And Simone's lips were on hers in a tender but possessive kiss.

A gasp rose from Jade's chest, tremors rippling through her, stirring desire deep in her core. She reached for Simone, clutching at the front of her blouse as the woman devoured her, her lips and tongue unyielding. Jade pressed her body back against Simone's, every part of her begging Simone to pull her closer, kiss her deeper, unravel her until there was nothing left.

Every part of her, except for the voice in the back of her mind warning her not to make the same mistake again.

Jade drew back, breaking the kiss. But her hands were still gripping Simone's blouse, and she didn't want to let go.

"I'm sorry." Jade shook her head. "I want this so badly, but I…"

Simone brought her hands up to Jade's, enveloping them with her own. "I know, Jade. I know. I shouldn't have kissed you. Not here, not now. But I can't fight it any longer."

Jade searched Simone's eyes. So she'd felt it too, all this time? That forbidden spark, that irresistible pull that Jade had been trying so hard to ignore?

Simone's hands tightened around hers. "I want you, Jade. And if you want me, I'll be at Club Velvet until midnight. Come to me there tonight. Or do nothing, and we'll pretend this never happened. We'll go back to being boss and employee, and I'll never bring this up again."

"And if I *do* go to the club tonight? What happens then?"

"Come to Club Velvet," Simone said, her voice dropping low, "and I'll make good on my offer to show you all the exquisite pleasures submission can bring."

Jade's heart raced. She'd turned Simone down once

before, and she'd regretted it ever since. She couldn't walk away again.

So why did she hesitate?

"The choice is yours. I'll be waiting for you, Jade." With one last piercing look, Simone released Jade's hands and returned to her desk, taking a seat behind it as if nothing had happened at all. "Now finish up here and go home."

Jade left Simone's office, her head spinning and her body alight. That kiss? It had awakened something in her, a need stronger than anything she'd ever felt before.

But the warning voice in the back of her mind remained. And it was too loud to drown out.

CHAPTER 10

S imone sat in Club Velvet's VIP lounge, drink in hand, watching the club below. The lounge was on a mezzanine above the main part of the club, surrounded by glass to provide a bird's eye view of the room so that Simone and the other owners could watch over it.

But tonight, Simone wasn't interested in what was going on inside the club. She was only interested in who walked through the door.

She'll show. Simone knew it. She'd known since the day Jade walked into her office that if she commanded it, Jade would come. But she needed it to be Jade's decision. She needed Jade to come to her.

"I wasn't expecting to see you tonight," a voice said.

Simone turned to see a woman at the top of the stairs. She was slender and willowy, with warm brown skin and tight, dark curls tied up at the top of her head, her stylish white pantsuit creating an elegant contrast with her skin.

"Valerie." Simone gave her a nod. "I wasn't expecting to

see you here, either." Between her daughter and her job as a Hollywood executive, Valerie's schedule was even busier than Simone's.

"Just stopped by after work to check on things. I'm not Madame V tonight." She took a seat next to Simone. "Are any of the others around?"

"Olivia is on a work trip. Elle is here, but last time I saw her she was preoccupied with a bratty brunette who probably has no idea what she's in for."

"The usual then." Valerie leaned back and crossed her legs. "I'm glad you're here because I have an idea for the club that I'd like to run by you."

As Valerie continued, Simone's attention drifted to the club's entrance. It was a weeknight, but the club was busy enough. In the last ten minutes alone, a dozen women had walked through the door.

But none of them were Jade.

"...we'd be running the events at a loss, but they have the potential to bring in a wider clientele." Valerie said. "Do we have the budget for it?"

"It won't be a problem," Simone murmured.

Valerie raised an eyebrow. "Did you hear a word I just said?"

"Beginner play parties. Once a month."

"So you *were* listening. But you obviously have something else on your mind." She glanced at Simone's face, then down at the entrance to the club. "Are you waiting for someone?"

Simone took a sip of her drink, an old fashioned. "Perhaps."

"And who is she?"

"A woman I met here on opening night. Who also happens to be my new assistant."

Valerie blinked. "You're serious?"

"Dead serious. I invited her back here tonight."

"You invited *your assistant* to Club Velvet?"

A voice rang out beside them. "I'm going to need you to start from the beginning, because that sounds juicy."

Simone turned to see Elle joining them at the table. She took a seat across from them, gathering her strawberry blonde hair over her shoulder and leaning in.

"So?" she said. "What's going on? I want to hear what has Madame V so scandalized."

"Simone invited her assistant here tonight," Valerie said. "Personally."

"Oh?" A smile spread across Elle's lips. "Is she cute?"

Simone gave her a sharp look. "Don't even think about it. She's off limits."

"Someone's feeling possessive." Elle swirled her drink around before raising her glass to her lips. "You must really be into this woman."

"I won't deny that. But it's nothing serious. It's purely physical."

Simone rarely let things go further than that. She'd had her share of lovers, but only a couple had lasted long enough to be considered girlfriends. One couldn't accept that for Simone, her career came first. The second dealt with that fact by having an affair with a coworker. It only confirmed what Simone had learned as a girl. Love was nothing more than a fantasy. Believing in it, indulging in it, was a weakness she couldn't afford.

"Whatever you do, tread carefully," Valerie said. "If you

get involved with your assistant and it gets out, it could turn into a scandal."

"Then we'll be careful that it doesn't get out," Simone said. "Not that anyone in the corporate world gives a damn. Half the execs in Los Angeles are having affairs with their secretaries."

"Just relax, Val," Elle chimed in. "I know you like to think you're everyone's mom and all, but Simone is a big girl. She'll be fine."

But Simone didn't hear what Elle said next. Because at that moment, a woman walked through the door to the club. A young woman, with long, dark hair and curves that teased and tempted her even from a distance. And while Simone couldn't see her face, she would recognize her anywhere.

Jade. She's come to me at last.

Elle's gaze flicked between Simone and the club's entrance. "That's her, isn't it?"

Simone said nothing, watching Jade as she slipped deeper into the club. She was still wearing the dress she'd worn to work, but she'd freed her hair from its ponytail, letting it flow down her back, just like the night they met. And just like the night at Simone's house, after she came out of the ensuite wrapped in Simone's bathrobe.

That entire night, and the morning that followed, Simone had fought to resist her attraction to her assistant, the chemistry simmering between them. But no more. Jade had made her choice.

She was Simone's to claim.

She rose to her feet. "It's been a pleasure catching up with you, ladies, but I need to go show someone the ropes."

She picked up her drink and swallowed what remained of it in one swig. She would show Jade what it meant to serve her in the most intimate of ways. She would give Jade the sweet surrender she desired.

But she would guard herself from anything more.

CHAPTER 11

J ade stood in the middle of the club, butterflies flitting in her chest. It had taken all of her willpower just to walk through the door.

She glanced toward the bar. A drink would help settle her stomach. But she needed to keep her head. And she needed to find Simone before she lost her nerve.

So why couldn't she move?

What would Renee do? After all, this was her kind of thing. If she were here, she'd give Jade the push she needed.

But Jade hadn't told Renee she was coming here tonight. She hadn't told Renee about the kiss. She could hardly believe it had happened herself.

She brought her fingers to her lips. She could still feel the echo of Simone's kiss on them, like it had only been moments ago. And she wanted to feel it all again. Simone's lips, her touch, the press of Simone's body against hers, the whisper of her voice in her ear as she tempted Jade with all kinds of wicked pleasures.

Jade glanced around the room. Everything Simone had

spoken of, everything in the club, was entirely new to her. She'd never been interested in any of it until the night she first set foot inside Club Velvet.

And now, Jade couldn't deny how much she was drawn to these seductive games of power and submission. She'd never had the chance to explore them before, never allowed herself to indulge in any kind of erotic fantasies. Sex and relationships? They were distractions she couldn't afford.

Living out those fantasies, with her boss, no less? What could possibly be more of a distraction, a risk? Jade had risked it all like this once before. And it had left her shattered.

It isn't too late. The door is right there—

Jade felt a hand on her shoulder. She spun around.

And came face to face with Simone.

"Hello, Jade," she said.

Jade's heart skipped. She opened her mouth to speak, but nothing came out.

Because suddenly, she was faced not with Simone, her boss, but with the woman she'd encountered at Club Velvet on opening night. The woman who had come to her rescue and swept her off her feet. The woman who had filled her mind with dreams of surrender.

The woman who had kissed her in her office barely a few hours ago.

"Simone," she said. "I…"

"Not here. Let's go sit down somewhere quiet so we can talk."

Simone placed a hand on Jade's lower back and led her through the club. Jade glanced around, electricity crackling through her from Simone's fingers all the way down into her core. Having Simone touch her so intimately in front of everyone felt deliciously forbidden.

"Here." Simone nodded at the purple velvet loveseat before them. "Sit."

Jade obeyed.

Simone took a seat next to her. "You're nervous. Why?"

"Why?" Jade gestured at the rest of the club. "There's all this, for starters. Like I said the night we met, I've never done anything like this before. And I don't have much experience with dating, let alone sex or anything more, and it's been a long time since I've been involved with anyone, and I don't think I'm ready for any kind of relationship—"

"Listen," Simone said. "If it was romance I wanted, would I have invited you to a place like this?"

"I guess not."

"Understand this, Jade. I don't want a girlfriend. I want a submissive."

A warm shiver rippled through Jade's body. Was that what she wanted to be to Simone? Was that what she yearned for every time she was in her boss's presence?

"And while this might all be new to you," Simone continued, "let me assure you that you're in experienced hands. I'm one of the owners of Club Velvet, after all."

Jade blinked. "Wait, what? *You own Club Velvet?*"

"Why do you think I was watching you on opening night? I was keeping an eye on the crowd, making sure everyone was enjoying themselves. Then I saw that woman harassing you."

"Oh. I guess I thought…" Jade lowered her gaze. Suddenly, that thought seemed silly.

But Simone read her mind. "Yes, that was why I helped you that night. That woman was making my club unsafe, and I couldn't allow it to happen. But that doesn't mean I didn't want you from the moment I laid eyes on you. That doesn't mean I haven't wanted you every moment since." She leaned in close, sliding a hand up Jade's thigh. "There's so much I want to show you."

Deep within Jade, desire flared. Her whole body begged for Simone to do just that, right here in front of everyone.

Instead, Simone drew back, crossing one leg over the other. "But before we begin, we have much to discuss. We need to set some boundaries and ground rules. To start with, all of this? It stays *outside* the office. It can't interfere with our work. And I can't afford to have half the office distracted by rumors and gossip."

Jade nodded. "Okay."

"And you should know, I'm a jealous Mistress. I don't like to share my toys. So if you're mine, you're mine alone, understand?"

Jade nodded again.

"Don't just nod," Simone said firmly. "Tell me you understand me."

"I understand," Jade said, her cheeks burning. 'Mistress Simone' wasn't all that different from the woman Jade worked for.

"Naturally, it goes both ways. You will be my one and only. And I will be yours."

Heat trickled through Jade's body at Simone's words. How was she going to keep everything between them contained while they were at work? She'd barely been able to keep herself together around Simone before tonight.

"Now, I want to talk about *you*," Simone said. "Tell me what you like."

Jade bit her lip. "I don't really know. There are so many

things I've thought about, dreamed about, especially after coming here the first time. But I've never tried any of it. I don't know what I really like."

"Then we'll have to find out together, won't we? And what better place to start than right here, tonight? Would you like that?"

"Yes." There was nothing Jade wanted more. Yet a part of her still had doubts.

"Know this," Simone said. "I won't be doing anything without your explicit consent. And you'll need a safeword. Do you have one?"

Jade shook her head.

"Let's go with something simple. 'Red' is your safeword. It means 'stop everything right now.' But if you just want me to slow down and check in with you, say 'yellow.' Then there's 'green.' I'm sure you can guess what that means. 'Keep going.'"

Jade nodded. Simone's concern for her—for what she liked, her comfort, her pleasure—was enough to silence all her hesitations. Simone wasn't anything like *her*. Simone was different.

And it would be different this time. Last time, with *her*, it had been a relationship. With *her*, it had been love, at least in Jade's eyes. But with Simone? It was pure, physical desire.

And as Jade looked back at her, she could see the same lust in Simone's eyes.

"Is there anything you'd like to say?" Simone said. "Anything you'd like to ask me? Don't be shy."

Jade shook her head. "No, nothing."

"Then let's go take a look at those private rooms." Simone stood up and held her hand out to Jade. "Come."

Pulse pounding, she placed her hand in Simone's.

Simone led her to a door to the side, a few steps away. Jade hadn't noticed it earlier. In the same black and purple wallpaper as the walls, it was camouflaged.

Simone produced a keycard and swiped it beside the door, opening it up. It led to another room with a dozen identical doors coming off it, each painted black with gold trim. All were shut. What was behind them?

"Over here." Simone led her to one of the doors on the right. "The private rooms still need some work, but this one is just about done."

Jade glanced at the door. Once she stepped through it, everything she'd spent weeks daydreaming about would become a reality.

Simone's eyes met hers. "Ready to go inside?"

Jade nodded confidently. "I'm ready."

Simone opened the door, holding it for Jade.

She took a deep breath.

And she stepped into the room.

CHAPTER 12

"Here we are," Simone said. "Our finest private room." Jade looked around. The room was lit faintly by a brass chandelier, the walls a shade of purple so dark it was almost black. And it was packed to bursting with all kinds of kinky furniture and equipment. A huge four-poster bed. A throne-like chair. A big wooden cross, padded and covered with black leather and shaped like an X. Jade had seen one just like it in The Playroom that first night.

But the rest of the equipment in the room was alien to her. There was a wooden contraption that looked like medieval stocks but had five holes. An elaborate metal frame a foot taller than her with rings hanging from it. A bench that resembled a saw horse, only with a triangular body and cuffs attached to the legs.

Are those ankle cuffs? Is someone supposed to sit on that? Jade's whole body tingled at the thought of the top edge of the bench digging between her thighs, her legs cuffed, with no way to escape—

"Like what you see, do you?" Simone asked.

Heat rose to Jade's skin. Was it that obvious?

"You haven't seen the half of it," Simone said. "There are so many toys in here for us to play with. So many wonderful tools of sensation and pleasure. Would you like me to show you?"

Jade nodded, hypnotized. "Yes."

Simone drew her over to the far wall. It was covered by a large black curtain spanning the entire length of the room. Leaving Jade standing before it, Simone walked over to a thick gold rope in the corner and gave it a firm tug.

Like magic, the curtain slid to one side, revealing the floor-to-ceiling shelves behind it. And for the second time that night, Jade found herself frozen in place.

Displayed on the shelves, illuminated by spotlights, was every kind of kinky toy and tool imaginable.

Simone stepped toward her, heels clicking on the polished floors. "Tell me." She slid her hand down Jade's back, drawing her closer to the shelves. "Tell me what you feel when you look at this."

"I feel..." Jade's voice quavered. "Curious. Excited. Exhilarated."

Simone drew a hand over the nearest shelf. On it was an array of blindfolds and gags in different shapes and materials, along with some rubber and metal objects that Jade didn't recognize.

"Tell me," Simone repeated. "Tell me what excites you. Tell me what you *desire*." She traced her fingertips over a thin leather blindfold. "Do you wish to be blindfolded, gagged, deprived of all your senses?"

Jade's pulse quickened. The thought alone was enough to set her nerves racing. But at the same time, it made her throb between her thighs.

Simone moved to the next shelf, running her fingers over each of the items on it. Coils of rope. Leather cuffs. Heavy metal shackles.

"Or do you long to be bound?" she asked. "Restrained and immobilized, helpless to resist your Mistress's sensual torment?"

Jade's heart thumped even faster. And with it, the ache between her legs deepened.

Simone slid her hand onto the next shelf, filled with all kinds of wicked-looking tools. Nipple clamps. Suction pumps. A tiny spiked wheel.

"Or perhaps it's sensation you crave. Pleasure, pain, everything in between." She swept her hand over to the next shelf, where a collection of whips, paddles, and canes were laid out. "Do you yearn for the thrill of a whip against your skin? The brush of a flogger? The sweet sting of a riding crop?"

Simone drew her fingers over the implements one by one, as if each were as precious as a diamond. Then she picked up the flogger, slapping it against her hand as she brought it back to where Jade stood.

"Tell me." She skimmed the tails of the flogger up Jade's shoulder and down her back. "What is it that you want?"

A shiver rolled through her. She turned to face Simone.

"No, don't look at me." She took Jade's chin between her fingers, tilting her face back to the shelves before them. "Look. Feel. Tell me what you desire."

Jade gazed straight ahead, her whole body ablaze. How could she think with Simone standing behind her, her body so close that Jade could feel its heat? How could she speak with Simone's lips at her ear, her breath caressing her neck?

"I want..." Jade drew in a deep breath and let it out slowly. "I want everything. I want to feel it all."

Simone stepped in even closer, her breasts brushing against Jade's back, the tails of the flogger tickling her bare arm.

"And I want to show you everything," she said. "Teach you and tame you, make you beg for more."

The flogger disappeared. And in its place was Simone's hand, gliding up Jade's arm, her shoulder, the side of her throat. Jade trembled, her body threatening to collapse under the weight of her own desire.

"I've been dreaming of all the sinful things I'm going to do with you," Simone said. "And now that I finally have you, I can do all those things and more."

From behind, she slid her hand down Jade's breasts, her stomach, her thighs. Jade let out a quivering breath, melting into Simone's body. Her fingertips burned through Jade's clothes, scorching her skin, igniting the spark in her core.

"But tonight," Simone said, her voice soft and low, "I just want *you*." She took the hem of Jade's dress, dragging it upwards, higher and higher until her panties were exposed. "I want to make you come undone. I want to feel you yield to me. I want you to pulse and throb at my fingers."

She slipped her hand between Jade's legs, stroking her through her panties. Jade's breath hitched. She was already wet.

"Is that what you want?" Simone said, sliding her other hand inside the top of Jade's dress, grasping at her breasts, grazing pebbled nipples with her fingertips. "Do you want me to unravel you?"

Jade's head fell back onto Simone's shoulder, her eyes falling shut. "God, yes."

A satisfied purr rose from Simone's chest. "You have no idea how much I want you."

Jade exhaled softly. And ever so slowly, Simone drew her hand back up and slipped it inside Jade's panties.

A moan fell from Jade's lips. She arched into Simone's hand, grinding back against her, urging her on. But Simone only tightened her grip around Jade's body, pulling her in closer.

"If you're going to be mine, I expect nothing less than your complete devotion." She slid her fingers down between Jade's lower lips, skating them over her folds. "I am your Mistress. I am your everything. Surrender to me."

A desperate whimper rose from Jade's chest. She wasn't bound, wasn't restrained in any way. Yet she was powerless to do anything but obey Simone. Powerless to resist her touch, her presence. Powerless against her own need.

Simone drew her fingers up to Jade's clit, skimming it with a fingertip. Jade gasped. She was so turned on that the slightest brush of Simone's fingertip sent tremors through her whole body.

"That's it," Simone crooned. "Just like that."

She moved her fingers between Jade's thighs, stroking and circling and teasing, her other hand playing at Jade's breasts under her dress. Jade shuddered and moaned, every sweep of Simone's fingers sending waves of pleasure through her, each more intense than the last.

"You're close, aren't you?" Simone said. "I can feel it."

Jade nodded, unable to speak.

"If you want me to let you come, you need to tell me who you belong to."

"You," Jade said, breathless. "You."

"That's right. From now on, you're mine to command.

No one touches you but me. No one pleasures you but me. You are *mine*."

"*Yes...*" Jade grasped blindly for Simone, one hand reaching back to grab her thigh, the other clamping onto Simone's arm at her chest, holding on tightly. She was so close now. So close!

"You're *mine*," Simone growled, her fingers moving faster between Jade's thighs. "You belong to me. You serve me. And if you serve me well? If you please me? I'll reward you with your every wicked desire."

"Yes," Jade cried. "Yes, yes!"

Her back arched, her mouth falling open as pleasure burst in her core. She bucked against Simone's body, holding onto her tightly as an unrelenting torrent of ecstasy rippled through her.

And when her orgasm faded, Simone reached up and turned Jade's head to face hers, kissing her soft but deep, tender but possessive. Just like Simone herself.

Just like her Mistress.

In the throes of her orgasm, their agreement had been sealed.

And there was no going back.

CHAPTER 13

"Sorry I'm late again." Jade sat down on the grass next to Renee. "I was doing something for Simone and lost track of time."

"No problem." Renee handed Jade her usual iced coffee and sandwich. "Here."

"Thanks, you're a lifesaver."

Jade unwrapped her sandwich and took a bite, then stretched her legs out in front of her, letting the sun's rays hit her skin. They'd decided to have lunch at the park today. The weather was perfect, and Jade wanted to enjoy it, especially since she finished work after the sun went down more often than not.

"How's the job going?" Renee asked.

Jade swallowed her food. "It's everything I hoped it would be. Not everything Simone has me doing is exciting, but I'm getting tons of experience. And Simone is a great boss."

She's great at other things, too. Jade couldn't stop thinking about that night at Club Velvet. In the days since, she'd replayed it over and over again in her mind. It only made her want more. Of Simone. Of the woman Simone was outside of the office. Of all the tantalizing things she'd promised to show her now that Jade was hers.

Renee raised an eyebrow. *"Simone is a great boss?* Last time I saw you, you were telling me how much of a hardass she is."

"I was being a little harsh," Jade said. "I was really stressed out that week. But things are better now. I got my car fixed, and everything with my apartment is finally sorted out. I managed to salvage most of my things, and my landlord is moving me to another studio in the same building."

"So no more cushy hotel room? I still can't believe your boss paid for that."

"She owns the hotel. It's not a big deal." Jade took a sip of her coffee. "I am going to miss that fancy suite though."

"Well, you definitely seem better than the last time I saw you. You're practically glowing. It's a little weird, actually."

"I'm just happy. There's nothing weird about that."

"No, it's not just that. There's something different about you." Renee narrowed her eyes. "Wait. Did you get laid?"

"God, Renee!" Jade glanced around. "Keep your voice down!"

"I'm not hearing a no. So you *did* get laid?"

"If I answer you, will you stop being so loud?"

Renee shrugged. "Sure."

"Fine, I got laid." Jade crossed her arms. "Are you happy?"

"I will be once you tell me about it."

Jade sighed. She wasn't getting out of this.

"Come on," Renee said. "I want *all* the details. Like who

she is, to start with. I didn't even know you were seeing someone."

"I wasn't. And I'm not. It's more of a casual thing."

But what had happened between them that night could hardly be described as *casual*. It had been so unbridled and raw, so intense.

"Really?" Renee studied Jade's face. "I didn't think 'casual' was your thing."

"I'm trying something new," Jade said. "And in more ways than one. Honestly, I can hardly believe I'm doing this myself."

"Doing what? And you still haven't told me who she is."

"Right. Well..." Jade pushed the ice in her coffee around with her straw. "Remember when I told you that the woman I met at Club Velvet turned out to be my boss?"

"Yes? And?" Renee's eyes widened. "Wait. *Wait.* You had sex with your boss?"

Jade nodded. "We went back to Club Velvet, and she showed me the private rooms. Turns out she's one of the club's owners, so we—"

Renee held up her hands. "Hold on a minute. You had sex in a private room at Club Velvet? With your boss? Who also owns the club?"

Jade nodded again.

"Holy..." Renee shook her head. "Am I really talking to Jade here? How many women have you even slept with? I don't think you've ever had a one-night stand before. And you banged *your boss?*"

"Well, yeah. And it wasn't a one-night stand. It's very much a no-strings thing, but it seems like we both want this to keep going."

Simone had made it clear that night. *You belong to me. You serve me. And if you serve me well? If you please me?*

I'll reward you with your every wicked desire.

"Right." Renee sipped her coffee thoughtfully. "Don't get me wrong. I'm glad you're finally getting some action. But are you sure this is a good idea?"

"Really?" Jade said. "You're the one who's always telling me to loosen up a little. That's what I'm doing."

"Yeah, but with your boss? Is that even allowed?"

"I don't know, but Simone owns the company. If she's not worried, I'm not. And we're keeping everything out of the office. During work hours, we're strictly professional."

Renee scoffed. "Yeah, like that'll last. Besides, even if you can keep the sex stuff separate from work, keeping your feelings separate from sex? That's a different story."

"You seem to manage fine. You have plenty of casual hookups."

"Yeah, but that's me. You're not the hookup type. You're the type who wants to fall madly in love on the first date, then move in together and adopt a bunch of cats."

Jade rolled her eyes. "That's not true."

"Oh yeah? Then how come every time anyone hits on you, you turn them down? You even turned Simone down at first. Face it, you're a romantic. You want more than hookups and flings. You want to be treated like a princess, showered with *I love yous* and thoughtful gifts. It's the way you've been since we first met. And there's nothing wrong with that."

"Maybe that's how I used to be, but I'm not like that anymore."

Jade had been a different person back then, young and optimistic, her head in the clouds. But having her heart crushed by someone she trusted, *loved*, had killed that part of her. That naïve girl didn't exist anymore.

"Look, I just don't want you getting hurt," Renee said. "You're one of my best friends. I can't help but worry about you."

"I know what I'm doing, Ree. I won't get hurt."

But was Renee right? Was getting involved with Simone, her boss, too risky?

Would things between them end the same way as they had with *her*?

No, because this time, Jade wasn't under any illusions about what was between her and Simone. And Jade was older now. Wiser. She knew to keep her guard up. She knew to keep her feelings in check.

Her phone buzzed. She took it from her purse to find a message from Simone.

Before you leave work today, come see me. I have something for you.

What could that possibly mean? A dozen possibilities flashed through her mind, each naughtier than the last.

"Who's making you blush like that?" Renee asked. "Was that Simone? I bet it was Simone."

"Maybe." Jade slipped her phone back into her purse. "She just wants to see me later, that's all."

"Uh-huh." Renee smirked. "Well, if she makes you smile like that, maybe I'm wrong about this. Maybe it isn't a bad idea. Just be careful, okay?"

"I will. I promise."

But that promise was as much to herself as to Renee. Because she wasn't going to let herself get hurt again.

And she wasn't going to lose herself in someone else again.

That evening, when Jade was ready to leave, she made her way to Simone's office. Inside, Simone sat behind her desk, flipping through a folder.

"I'm about to head home," Jade said. "You wanted to see me?"

Simone shut the folder and set it aside. "Now that you've finished work for the day, you're officially off the clock. Which means I can give you this." She opened the top drawer of her desk and produced a document. "It's a questionnaire."

Jade took the questionnaire from Simone. As she read the title on the first page, her face grew warm. She glanced over her shoulder. Thankfully, she'd remembered to shut the door.

"This is a way for me to understand your desires, your interests," Simone said. "Along with your limits. While we touched upon these subjects the other night, when it comes to consent and communication, there's no room for ambiguity. Especially in an arrangement like ours. This will make it clear to me what you're comfortable with and what you aren't."

Jade flipped through the questionnaire. There were dozens of pages, covering every erotic practice imaginable in intimate detail. Every possible sex act, from vanilla to extreme. All kinds of kinky activities, from bondage to impact play. Each took up a page on its own, with a question for every different toy and tool.

And as the questions went on, the kinks and fetishes became more obscure. Pet play. Electroplay. Chastity belts.

Jade hadn't even heard of half of them before. *What the hell is a vacuum bed?*

"Any activities you like or want to try, mark the 'yes' column," Simone continued. "Anything that's a hard limit, mark 'no.' For anything in between that you might want to try but are unsure about, mark 'maybe.' That includes any soft limits, which are things you may be willing to do with negotiation and discussion."

Jade nodded. Hard limits, soft limits, negotiation. It was enough to make her head spin. It was just like Simone to give her what amounted to kinky homework.

"None of your answers will be set in stone," Simone said. "You can change your mind at any time, just say the word. It's only natural that your tastes will change the more we explore. And regardless of your answers, we *will* be taking it slow. You're too inexperienced to know your limits, so I'm not going to throw you in the deep end, understand?"

"I understand." Jade couldn't deny that Simone's careful, considerate approach reassured her. At the same time, no small part of her longed to jump into the deep end with Simone.

But that was dangerous. She was already taking a chance in trusting Simone. She had to keep her head.

"Take your time filling it out. *At home*, might I add. This conversation aside, we do not mix work and play." Simone leaned forward, her eyes locking onto Jade's. "And I'm very much looking forward to playing with you."

Heat rose through Jade's body. How was it that Simone could make her come apart with just a look and a few words?

How was Jade supposed to work alongside her every day without falling to pieces?

Simone's lips curled into a slight smile. "I'll see you tomorrow, Jade."

Jade mumbled a goodbye, slipping the questionnaire into her bag as she left the office. Her body still burned as she made her way down to the parking garage beneath the building, where her car was parked in the space reserved for Simone's assistant.

She slipped into her car. As she set her bag on the passenger seat, the questionnaire slid out of the top and fell down into the footwell.

Jade picked it up. There was no harm in taking another peek at it before she got home. As she flipped through the questionnaire, she imagined herself with Simone, doing each of the activities within its pages. Some made her heart race, her body sizzle. Some made her squirm in her seat at just the thought.

But others made her hesitate. *Blindfolds. Gags.* Both excited her. At the same time, the idea of not being able to see anything, or say anything, was anxiety-inducing. She'd be completely at Simone's mercy. And that was a level of trust she could never see herself having in another person.

'No' to blindfolds and gags. And 'no' to anything to do with extreme pain.

But spanking and impact play? Those were a definite *yes.* She didn't know why they appealed to her. But she could still feel the way her body flooded with heat when Simone showed her all those whips in the private room that night, describing each sensation they created. *The thrill of a whip against your skin... the brush of a flogger... the sweet sting of a riding crop...*

A gentle ache grew between Jade's legs. She closed her

eyes, sinking into her seat. Her hand crept down her stomach, over her pants, down to where her thighs met—

The chatter of voices echoed through the parking garage. Jade opened her eyes, glancing at her rearview mirror to see a pair of women stroll by.

Snapping herself out of her trance, Jade tossed the questionnaire onto the passenger seat. But as she started her car and pulled out of the parking lot, her mind raced with thoughts of all the enticing things Simone had to teach her.

CHAPTER 14

It was the moment Simone had been waiting for. No, the moment she had orchestrated. After weeks—months—of negotiations, she had a meeting with Ashton herself to discuss the acquisition of The Ashton Star.

And all she could think about was Jade.

Jade, the moment they'd kissed in her office and she'd dissolved at the touch of Simone's lips. Jade, in the private room at Club Velvet, entranced by everything around her. Jade, coming apart in her arms, her head tipping back as she pulsed against Simone's fingers, quivering in orgasmic bliss.

Jade, pledging herself to her, proclaiming *I belong to you.*

She glanced at Jade in the seat next to her, her laptop in front of her, eager and ready as always. *She'd look better at my feet.* Simone had told herself she wouldn't mix business with pleasure, but with every day that passed, the temptation was becoming harder to resist.

Focus. It was bad enough that her meeting with Ashton had been changed to a phone call at the last minute. Simone couldn't afford for it to be derailed any further.

She turned her attention to the voice echoing through the conference room speaker. It belonged to Ashton's nephew and her current COO, Evan.

"Thank you again for agreeing to this change of plans," he said. "Apologies for the late notice."

"I was looking forward to speaking with Ashton in person, but this will suffice," Simone said. "When will she be joining us?"

Evan cleared his throat. "Yes, about that. There's been another change of plans. Ashton is unable to join us today. I will be representing her instead."

Simone held back a curse. She'd already had countless meetings with Evan and Ashton's other executives, all of which had been fruitless. If she was going to get her hands on The Ashton Star, she needed to talk to Ashton herself.

"I trust Ashton is well?" Simone asked.

"She is," Evan replied. "She is simply unavailable at present."

Simone leaned back in her chair and crossed her arms. Another negotiation tactic? Another roadblock dropped in her way? She'd already dealt with all the others. Her few competitors had balked at the price of fixing the defects under the building. Orion Development was still in the running, but with an insultingly low offer. Simone was the only real player left.

But she still had to deal with Ashton's nephew and the lackeys whispering into his ear, telling him when to buy and sell, when to give ground and when to play hardball.

But playing hardball was Simone's forte.

She rose to her feet. "If Ashton is unavailable, we'll reschedule for a time when she *is* available. I'll have my assistant get in touch."

Her words had the desired effect. "I assure you, I'm more than capable of handling any negotiations in Ashton's stead," Evan said.

Simone began pacing beside the conference room table. "I don't see what there is left to negotiate. My offer is on the table. We've discussed every last detail of it. It's time to seal the deal."

"I understand that you're eager to see this done, but Ashton is not yet satisfied with your terms."

"Then she can speak to me about that herself," Simone said.

"Ashton is a busy woman. It's my job to ensure we have your best and final offer before we present it to—"

"Cut the bullshit, Evan. We both know I'm the only player left. My offer is more than fair, especially given those defects that were buried in the building report. This is the best deal you're going to get."

"I wouldn't be so sure. We're still in talks with Orion Development. They've put in a very appealing offer."

Simone stifled a sigh. Evan was bluffing, and badly.

Two can play that game.

"You know what?" Simone said. "If Orion's offer is so appealing, *take it.*"

There was a pause at the other end of the line. "I'm sorry?"

"You heard me. Take the deal. Sell The Ashton Star to a faceless corporation that will raze it to the ground to build a parking lot. Wipe the Ashton family legacy from the city. Because what does it matter, as long as you get to line your pockets?"

Beside her, Jade's mouth fell open, a mixture of shock and admiration in her eyes. *You like it when I play hardball too, do you?* Slipping behind her, Simone leaned her arms on the top of Jade's chair, letting her hand fall to her assistant's shoulder, her fingertips grazing her bare neck. All it would take was a word, and she could have Jade right here, right now, pinned to the conference room table so that Simone could explore every one of those delectable curves...

"Excuse me?" Evan's shrill voice echoed through the speaker. "You can't speak to me like that! Ashton will be hearing about this!"

"Good," Simone said. "Tell her what I said. Tell her she can sell The Ashton Star to Orion Development for easy money. Or she can sell it to me and know that I'll make sure the hotel her family poured themselves into for generations remains standing for decades to come."

"You think we're going to sell you the hotel now? After you insult me like—"

A woman's voice interrupted him, clear and crisp. "Oh, shut up, will you?"

Simone straightened up, exchanging a glance with Jade. There was another person on the call.

"You tried to play her, and she played you instead," the voice said. "And quite frankly, you deserved it. To think I paid for you to go to business school."

Jade's brows drew together in confusion. But Simone already knew who the voice belonged to.

"Hello, Ashton," she said. "It's good to finally speak to you."

"Same to you. You're quite the businesswoman, Ms. Weiss. I apologize for my nephew's behavior. He's still learning the ropes. And I apologize for the subterfuge. I simply wanted to get a sense of just the kind of person I'm dealing with."

"I don't appreciate games, Ashton. Do not test me again."

Jade's eyes widened in shock. But Simone hadn't come as far as she had by becoming a pushover.

"I won't," Ashton said. "You've proven yourself to be as formidable as everyone says. But if I'm to decide whether to leave The Ashton Star in your hands, I'll have to meet you in person."

"Just name the time and place," Simone said.

"Next week, Friday. Dinner at The Ashton Star. It will give you a chance to see the hotel in its current form. And I'll make the penthouse suite available for you to stay in so you'll get the full Ashton Star experience."

Simone turned to Jade. "I'll have my assistant clear my schedule. And I'll be bringing her along to assist me. I trust you'll be able to accommodate her."

"I'll make the necessary arrangements," Ashton said. "In the meantime, if anything comes up, I'll have my nephew give you my direct contact number."

"I appreciate it. It's been a pleasure speaking with you."

Simone nodded to Jade, who reached for the speaker in the center of the table and ended the call with the press of a button.

"Come, let's go back to my office." Simone had taken the meeting in the conference room out of habit, but now that it was done, she needed to get Jade alone, somewhere more private.

Her assistant gathered her laptop and files in her arms and followed Simone out the door.

"I'll need you to reschedule all my appointments next Friday and Saturday," Simone said. "Move the meeting with the Silver Lake contractor to this Friday so we can get it over with."

Jade nodded. "Right away."

Simone continued to fire off instructions as they made their way back to her office. But as soon as they were inside, she shut the door and backed Jade against it, a hand on either side of her head, pinning her in place.

Jade exhaled softly, surprise and desire swirling in her eyes.

"What was that in there, hm?" Simone said.

Jade hugged her laptop to her chest. "What was what?"

"The way you kept looking at me. Like you were begging me to drag you into the storage closet and fuck you while the whole office listened."

Jade's cheeks turned the same shade of pink as her lips. "I-I don't know what you mean."

"Oh, I think you do. You're looking at me the same way right now. It's utterly distracting." Simone traced a finger along Jade's collarbone, up the curve of her throat, all the way to her chin. "I ought to make you kneel beside my desk for the rest of the day as punishment."

Jade trembled, her lips parting silently. Satisfaction rippled through Simone's body. If she were to order Jade to do just that, she'd be on her knees within seconds.

"But I don't mix work and play," Simone said. "And we have far too much work to do. We only have a week and a half until dinner with Ashton, and we need to prepare. Things in the office are going to become even more intense. My question is, can you handle the heat?"

Jade nodded. "Whatever you need," she said softly.

"I'll have your desk moved into my office so we can work together more... intimately. And don't you worry. I'll be sure to reward you for all your hard work in a way you'll appreciate. Especially now that you've given me the questionnaire back and I know exactly what you like." Simone dropped her voice to a whisper. "Your answers were very illuminating. Who knew you were into such filthy things?"

Jade shifted against the door, the flush on her cheeks deepening to crimson. Simone hadn't needed to read Jade's answers to the questionnaire to know how much it turned her on to be teased and toyed with. And watching her blush and squirm only stoked the flames burning within Simone.

But they were at work. And Simone had already stepped too far over the line.

She straightened up, releasing Jade. "It's time for your lunch break. Take your time, get something to eat. Because when you get back, our work truly begins."

Jade nodded. But as she turned and opened the door, she hesitated.

"Is something the matter?" Simone asked.

"No, I just have a question," Jade said. "Back there, in the meeting. How did you know that would work? Telling Evan to take the other offer?"

"I'll admit that I wasn't expecting it to work as quickly as it did. I expected that Evan would go crying to his aunt about what I said. He's just the type to do that. It was pure luck that Ashton was listening in."

"But why did you say everything you said in the first place?"

"It's simple. Deals like these? They're never only about money. It isn't simply a matter of who's the highest bidder. Humans aren't machines. We're driven by emotion, for better and for worse. We have our own individual wants and needs. Understanding what someone really wants can be the difference between closing a deal or not."

"And that's what Ashton wants?" Jade asked. "Her family's legacy to continue? How did you know that?"

"It was a calculated guess. You see, Ashton has been making some major changes to her company recently. Although she's only in her forties, there's speculation that she's planning to retire soon. She's been training Evan to be her successor, but rumor has it that she's concerned about his performance. She's worried about the future of her family's company, its reputation, the legacy she'll leave behind. Appealing to that was the smart play."

"That makes sense. Still, it seems like a big risk to take."

"It was a gamble, yes. But sometimes, you need to take those risks. Sometimes, you need to trust your instincts and take that leap."

Jade nodded. "I understand, I think."

"Good. Now, go to lunch."

Jade left the room, shutting the door behind her. Simone returned to her desk, taking a seat behind it and stretching out in her chair. What the two of them were doing? Letting the lines blur? That was a risk.

But Jade was worth the risk. Simone had never wanted anyone so intensely. No one else had lit a fire within her the way Jade did.

And what harm was there in embracing that? After all, it was only a game. A deliciously twisted game of power and control.

And it had only just begun.

CHAPTER 15

Simone unlocked her front door and ushered Jade inside. "Finally. I couldn't spend another minute in that office."

Jade readjusted the box of files and folders in her arms. It was late on Friday afternoon, and she and Simone had left the office for a change of scenery. But they still had plenty to do.

Jade gazed around the mansion. It was just as breathtaking as it had been the first time Simone brought her here. "This is definitely better than working in the office. If I lived here, I'd never leave."

Simone walked over to the cherry wood dining table and set the box she was carrying down on it, gesturing for Jade to do the same. "It has its perks. It almost makes that godawful traffic worth it."

"You've never thought about living downtown instead? Somewhere closer to the office?"

"I've considered it. Actually, I was days away from closing on a condo downtown when I found this place. The moment I stepped through the door, I knew I had to make it my own."

"I can see why." Jade wandered over to the glass doors leading out onto the deck. It was evening and the sun was setting, the sky above the city painted purple and orange. "It's beautiful."

Simone slipped behind her, drawing her hand up the back of Jade's arm. "Yes," she said. "It is."

A shiver rolled through Jade's body. While they weren't in the office any longer, they were still on the clock. Did that mean keeping things strictly professional between them?

Simone swept her hand along the back of Jade's shoulder. "It's been such a long day. I could use a drink. Would you like one?"

Jade nodded. "Sure."

"Have a seat. I'll take care of everything." Simone sauntered over to a large antique wooden cabinet near the dining table. Inside was a minibar, stocked generously with top-shelf liquors and crystal glasses. "What would you like?"

"Whatever you're having is fine."

As Jade sat down at the table, Simone set about making some kind of cocktail. Jade watched, hypnotized by every movement of Simone's hands, by the delicate way she handled each tool, each ingredient. And as she took a long-handled spoon, stirring gently, Jade saw, in her mind, Simone caressing the handle of the flogger she'd held that night at Club Velvet.

Jade bit the inside of her cheek, trying to stem her growing desire. How was she going to concentrate on work for the rest of the evening when it was just the two of them, all alone in Simone's mansion?

Simone divided the contents of the cocktail shaker between two long-stemmed glasses, garnishing each with a cherry on a metal toothpick. Then she brought the glasses over to the dining table, handing one to Jade.

"A Manhattan," Simone said, raising her glass to her lips.

Jade followed suit, taking a generous sip of her drink, relishing the slight burn of the whiskey in her throat. She'd never had a Manhattan before, but she liked it.

"Now, I'm going to go get out of these stifling clothes," Simone said. "While you wait, sort through these boxes and find the development plans for me."

As Simone disappeared upstairs, Jade reached into the box in front of her and grabbed a handful of files. Simone didn't seem interested in anything other than work this evening. But that didn't stop Jade from picturing her boss upstairs in her bedroom, kicking off her heels, slipping out of her dress, her bra tossed aside to reveal her bare breasts...

Jade picked up her drink and took a long swig, fortifying herself as she began searching through the files. But five minutes and half a glass later, she still hadn't found what she was looking for.

"Hard at work as ever, I see."

Jade spun around. Simone was standing just a few feet away, but she'd been so engrossed in her search that she hadn't noticed her.

Jade was certainly noticing her now. Simone had swapped out her work clothes for a pale silk robe, belted at the waist, the same robe she'd worn the morning after she brought Jade to her mansion for the first time. And she was still wearing her heels.

Simone sashayed over to where Jade stood. "Do you have

any idea how hard this has been? Having you in my office every single day, without being able to so much as touch you?"

Jade's heart began to pound. Simone had let her hair down, her long blonde locks cascading over her shoulders. But it did little to soften the intensity of her expression, the hunger in her gaze.

Her eyes never leaving Jade's, Simone reached around her, picking up her own drink from the dining table. She took a long sip, leaving a ruby-red lip print behind on the rim of the glass.

"You've been taunting me," she said, "*tempting me*, all day long. And now? Now, I finally get to give you what you so desperately need."

"I…" Jade glanced at the files on the table behind her. "I haven't found those development plans yet."

She cursed to herself. Why had she said that? Work was the last thing on her mind, but Simone had her too flustered to think straight. It didn't help that she could see the faint outline of lacy lingerie under Simone's robe.

"Forget the plans. They don't matter. What matters is that I want you, right here, right now. But first…" Simone plucked the toothpick from her drink, slipping it into her mouth and sucking the cherry from it. "You've been teasing me all week. I think a little punishment is in order."

Punishment? What did Simone mean by that?

Why was Jade suddenly so eager to find out?

She lowered her gaze, peering up at Simone from underneath her eyelashes. "If that's what you think, Mistress."

The slightest hint of a smile crossed Simone's lips. She plucked Jade's drink from her hand and set both their glasses down on the antique cabinet before turning back to Jade.

"Turn around," she said. "And put your hands behind your back."

Jade turned to face the dining table. Her pulse raced. She'd obeyed Simone's order without question, without thought. Why did her body react to Simone that way? Why did Jade yearn to obey her, to serve her, to be *used* by her? It didn't make sense. But at the same time, it felt natural.

And the moment Simone's hands touched her wrists, every thought in her mind crumbled to dust. She was under Simone's spell, hers to command. And she wanted nothing more.

Simone drew Jade's wrists together behind her back. "Keep your hands like that."

A second later, something cool and silky-smooth touched her wrists. *Is Simone tying my hands together?*

Jade didn't dare turn and look. But she could feel the silken rope tighten around her wrists, could feel it twist and tug as Simone tied a firm knot. And when she was done, Jade pulled at her wrists experimentally, but the rope held fast.

Simone spoke from behind her, her lips tickling Jade's ear. "Now I have you just the way I want you."

Jade's breath trembled. She turned to face Simone. Her robe was wide open now, the silk belt tied around Jade's wrists. And underneath the robe, Simone wore a lacy bra and matching panties in a dark crimson, rich and deep against her pale skin.

"Did I tell you to turn around?" Simone asked.

Jade's cheeks flushed. "No."

"Then turn back around."

Jade did as she was told. Why did Simone's rebukes make her just as hot as the woman's praise did?

But Simone's next command made her even hotter. "Bend over the table."

Jade leaned her body on the table, the hard wood cool against the side of her face. But inside, she burned.

"Look at you," Simone said. "Presented to me on a silver platter, ready and waiting. I've been daydreaming about having you in my office, just like this. Bending you over my desk, taking you in every way imaginable." She trailed her fingertips down Jade's neck, her shoulder. "Oh, I'm going to have so much fun with you, princess."

Jade's breath hitched. "What are you going to do with me?"

Simone snaked her hand down to Jade's ass, stroking it through her skirt. "Isn't it obvious?"

"You mean... you're not going to use a whip or anything?"

"Not tonight. You're not ready for that yet."

"Oh. Right."

"Are you actually disappointed?" Simone asked, amusement clear in her voice.

"Maybe a little," Jade admitted.

"You've been dreaming about that, haven't you? Dreaming of my whip against your skin? I've been dreaming about that too."

Simone slid her hand down further, down to the hem of Jade's skirt. Hooking her fingers underneath it, she dragged it up to Jade's hips, exposing her thighs to the cool air. Jade's skin tingled, desire shooting straight between her legs.

"But like I told you, we're taking it slow," Simone said. "There will be no whips and toys tonight. And I don't need them. All it takes to make you come apart is the simple idea of being bound and powerless, subject to my every whim. Whether that be for punishment or *pleasure*."

She drew her hand up the inside of Jade's thigh, tracing her fingers between Jade's lower lips through her panties. Jade shivered. Was she wet already?

"Tell me," Simone said. "How does it feel to be at my mercy?"

Jade quivered. She could barely think, let alone speak. But somehow, she managed to utter a single word.

"Green."

Simone laughed softly. "Eager, are we? All right."

She drew Jade's skirt all the way up to her waist, leaving her ass thrust in the air, her thin panties offering little protection. The throbbing between her thighs deepened, anticipation swelling inside her.

Simone skimmed her hands over Jade's ass cheeks. "Do you know why naughty little things like you enjoy being punished?"

"No," Jade said quietly.

"Because sometimes, punishments can be pleasurable. Sometimes, the anticipation, the build-up, all those sinful feelings that come with it, can be as intoxicating as pleasure itself."

Simone's hand disappeared from Jade's ass. She squeezed her eyes shut, her heartbeat thundering in her ears.

Not a second later, Simone's hand met Jade's ass cheek in a firm but measured smack. She jolted against the table. It barely hurt, but it made her sizzle all over.

Simone drew her hands over Jade's ass again, soothing her stinging cheeks. "And the pain that comes with it? The after-burn? That's all part of what makes punishments so delicious. Sometimes, that pain can make you feel more alive than sex."

She spanked Jade again, harder this time. A gasp spilled from her lips, the hot sting of the impact spreading across her skin. But Simone didn't give her a moment to breathe before bringing her hand down again, once, twice, three times, on one ass cheek then the other.

Jade hissed through her teeth, her whole body tensing. That had hurt. But as Simone continued, raining spanks over the backs of Jade's ass and thighs, she felt a pleasant warmth flooding her body, penetrating deep into her.

Is this starting to feel... good?

Jade relaxed against the table, bound hands settling in the small of her back. Simone spanked over and over again, each impact harder than the last. And each impact set off a spark inside Jade's core until she felt like she was going to explode.

"You feel it, don't you?" Simone said. "That rush of adrenaline and endorphins? The way the pain transforms into bliss?"

Jade squirmed against the table. "Mmhm."

"That's what makes this so enticing. And not only for you. The sight of you writhing around on my dining table is one I'll never forget."

She slid her hands up the backs of Jade's thighs, her ass cheeks. Jade purred, Simone's touch soothing her burning skin.

"Of course, punishments like these aren't always fun and games," Simone said. "They can also be used for discipline. There's nothing like a good spanking to keep a bratty, disobedient submissive in line. But I won't need to do that with you, will I?"

Jade shook her head, her cheek pressed against the table.

Suddenly, Simone's hand hit her ass in a firm smack. Jade exhaled sharply, the impact rippling through her in the most delectable way.

"I asked you a question. I expect you to answer it." Simone leaned down, speaking into her ear. "You'll be good, won't you? I won't need to keep you in line?"

"No," Jade said, breathless. "I'll be good."

"That's right." Simone delivered another solid slap to Jade's ass cheek. "And good girls? They get rewarded with all kinds of wonderful things."

She slid her hand down between Jade's legs, pushing the now-soaked fabric of her panties between her lower lips. A moan erupted from Jade's chest. She was even more sensitive now than before.

"I can tell you're at your limit in more ways than one," Simone said. "Had enough?"

Jade nodded, then remembered Simone's words. "Yes."

"Then get up. Let me see your face."

Her hands still bound behind her back, Jade levered herself up and turned to face Simone. Her ass and thighs ached, but that only deepened the desire inside her.

Simone reached up, cradling Jade's cheek in her hand. "You did well, princess."

Jade trembled. The way Simone was looking at her, her eyes alight with a mixture of affection and lust, made her whole body pulse.

"And now," Simone said, "it's time for your reward."

CHAPTER 16

Simone took Jade by the waist, drawing her into a hot, hard kiss. It was the first time Simone had kissed her since that night at Club Velvet. And just like that night, it filled Jade with a desperate need.

A begging murmur rose from her chest. Simone deepened the kiss, her lips growing more demanding as she pinned Jade against the hardwood table, the edge of the tabletop digging into her thighs. Jade reached out to draw her closer, but her hands were bound behind her back. All she could do was pull vainly at her bonds, urging Simone on with her lips, pleading with her.

Simone pressed her body against Jade's, her breasts soft under silk and lace. Her thigh slipped between Jade's legs, stoking the fire between them. Jade ground her hips against her, a whimper rising from her chest.

"Simone," she said. "*Simone—*"

She stifled Jade's pleas with a kiss, her hands roaming down the front of her chest. Her fingers worked at the buttons of Jade's blouse, one by one, until all were undone.

Tearing it open, Simone ran her hands up Jade's bare stomach, caressing her breasts before pulling down the cups of her bra, exposing them completely.

Jade's breath quickened, her nipples tightening into peaks. She'd only been intimate with one woman before, only ever shown this much of her body to one other person. Usually, the thought alone was enough to make Jade feel self-conscious.

But with Simone gazing back at her, desire smoldering in her eyes, she felt nothing but *need*.

"You," Simone whispered, drawing her fingers along Jade's breasts with a feather-light touch. "You're perfection."

Jade let out a quivering breath. Simone swept her fingertips over Jade's nipples, shooting heat straight into her core. Just the slightest touch of Simone's fingers made her tremble and gasp. It was the sweetest torture.

Without warning, Simone grabbed hold of Jade's hips, hoisting her up onto the edge of the dining table. Her ass and thighs were still tender, but it only inflamed her more. As Simone pushed herself between Jade's thighs, she spread her legs out wide. With her hands tied behind her back, she was powerless to do anything more.

"This is what I've always liked about you," Simone purred. "Always so willing, so pliant. Always so ready for me."

She slid her hands up to the waistband of Jade's panties. Jade lifted her hips, one side after the other, as Simone drew the panties down her thighs, all the way to her ankles.

Tossing them aside, she pushed Jade's knees apart again. Then she slipped a hand between Jade's thighs, fingers skating over her clit, skimming up and down her folds.

She circled Jade's entrance with a fingertip. "Do you want me inside you?"

"God, yes," Jade said. "I need you—"

Before she could say another word, Simone slipped a finger inside, then another. Jade gasped, her hands curling into fists behind her back as Simone slid in deeper, filling her completely. Jade's eyes fell shut, a tremor spreading through her. And as Simone began moving inside her, the tension in her body melted away, replaced by pure, unrelenting pleasure.

A moan rose from Jade's chest, her back and hips arching toward Simone.

"That's it," she said, her lips grazing Jade's ear. "Come apart for me."

She moved her fingers faster, curling them against that sweet spot inside, the heel of her hand rolling over Jade's aching clit. And with every thrust, a jolt of electricity coursed through her, rocking her body and the table underneath her. A folder slid from the tabletop onto the floor, its contents spilling out. But Jade hardly noticed. She was so lost in sensation, lost in Simone and the pleasure deep between her thighs, building and building like a gathering storm.

She wrapped her legs around Simone's hips, thighs clenching, hips rocking, until finally, she couldn't take it any longer.

"Oh god…" Jade's whole body tensed. "Oh!"

Her climax hit her like a crashing wave, surging through her body. Her head flung back, a cry rising from her chest as ecstasy consumed her. But Simone didn't stop, thrusting and delving and curling her fingers, drawing Jade's orgasm on and on.

Until finally, she fell back down to the table, breathless, sweaty, and spent.

$$\sim$$

"Here." Simone handed Jade a glass of water. "Drink."

She waited for Jade to finish the entire glass before taking it from her and setting it down on the coffee table. Then she took a seat on the couch next to Jade, drawing her down into her lap, her arms draped around her.

Jade closed her eyes and let out a contented sigh. She liked this warmer, softer side of Simone. How many people got to see this side of the formidable Simone Weiss?

"That was amazing," Jade murmured. "I'm glad you decided we should spend the evening here instead of in the office." She peered up at Simone. "Was that just an excuse to get me back here so you could... you know?"

"Not entirely," Simone said. "We do need to get some work done this evening. But I thought we could both use the chance to unwind."

Jade smiled. "Glad I could help. But if we need to get back to work—"

"Oh, I'm not done with you yet. Besides, I'd be remiss in my duties as your Mistress if I didn't give you some aftercare."

"Right," Jade said. "I had to look up what that word meant, along with a bunch of words from that questionnaire. My search history is filled with things like 'what is forniphilia?' now."

Simone chuckled softly. "I can't say that's a personal kink of mine, but we've discussed getting someone in for a demonstration at the club. We want to cater to all kinds of tastes."

Jade studied Simone's face. "The way you talk about all this. It's like it's so mundane to you."

"I wouldn't say it's mundane. But it's a world I'm intimately familiar with."

"So how long have you been into this kind of thing?" Jade asked.

"It's hard to say. I've been drawn to it all my entire life. Domination, submission, everything that comes with it. But all the trappings? The whips, and cuffs, and ropes, and so on? They're just tools. Props. There's satisfaction in mastery, in wielding those tools with an expert hand. But that's not what it's about for me. That's not what really appeals to me."

"Then what does?"

"What really gives me satisfaction?" Simone said. "It's submission in its purest form. A woman on her knees, at my feet, surrendering every part of her being to me. That level of vulnerability, of trust, is a transcendental experience. It's the most beautiful gift a submissive can give her Domme."

Jade's heart raced. The erotic games the two of them played left her feeling vulnerable. But the surrender Simone spoke of? The trust? That seemed like something different. Something *more*.

"Is that why you started Club Velvet?" Jade asked. "Because of your love of BDSM?"

Simone nodded. "I wanted to create a place where women are free to explore all our deepest, darkest desires. Or rather, *we* wanted to. While the idea was mine, the club was made possible with the help of some like-minded friends."

"The other owners, right? I heard the club was started by a bunch of rich lesbians, but that's all."

"Well, there are one or two bisexuals in the mix, but that's the gist of it. There are four of us, each playing our own role. I'm the unofficial CEO, dealing with the big picture. Elle handles most of the logistics of running the club, since that's her area of expertise. Olivia does PR and deals with people. Valerie? She holds us all together, makes sure everything is running smoothly. Between her kid and her job as a Hollywood exec, she has plenty of experience with averting disasters."

"Wait a minute," Jade said. "Are you talking about *Valerie Kane*? The movie producer?"

"That's right."

"Wow." Valerie Kane was practically Los Angeles royalty. Then again, so was Simone. "How do you even have time for all this? Running the club as well as your company?"

"I have help. Like my brilliant assistant."

Simone leaned down and kissed Jade on the forehead. As Jade snuggled against her, she caught a glimpse of the files on the dining table. Simone had insisted on bringing them home for the weekend so she could prepare for their dinner with Ashton.

"Do you really need to spend the weekend going through all those files?" Jade asked. "You already know every little detail of what's in them."

"Perhaps," Simone said. "But this is important. I need to be thorough."

"Why is this deal so important to you in the first place? There are plenty of other hotels in LA. And you own half of them already. Your company is booming, and you've made a ton of profitable acquisitions in the last year alone. Why focus so much on acquiring The Ashton Star? Especially since it's such a risky investment?"

Simone peered down at Jade. "I didn't know you were so familiar with my company's affairs. All of this falls far outside of your job description."

"I don't plan on being an assistant forever," Jade said. "I want a career of my own, just like yours. That's why I wanted this job; to learn from the best. I did as much research as I could on you and your company before I even applied."

"I shouldn't be surprised. My assistant chose you for a reason. And *I* chose you for a reason. There aren't many women who would beg me to fuck them and ask me to explain my business acquisitions afterward."

Jade's face flushed, eliciting a smile from Simone.

"But your assessment of The Ashton Star acquisition is correct," she said. "It *is* a high-risk investment. But that doesn't mean it's a bad investment. Given enough time, I can turn it around. It will be a challenge, but I'll make it happen."

"But why go through all that trouble? What makes The Ashton Star worth it?"

Simone's hand fell to Jade's arm. "I'm not usually one for sentiment, but there's a part of me that's simply drawn to The Ashton Star. It has so much history, so much life. It's stood the test of time, generation after generation. There's something appealing about that."

That wasn't the answer Jade was expecting. But if there was one thing she'd noticed about her boss, it was that she had an appreciation for old things. And it had been Simone who said that humans were driven by emotion, first and foremost. Why would she be any different?

"I want to turn The Ashton Star into something that reflects the spirit of Los Angeles," Simone said. "The city of dreams, a city of endless possibilities. LA has always been my home. The Ashton Star is its heart. I want to make it shine again."

Jade gave her a soft smile. "I understand that. That's why I moved to LA in the first place. Well, I moved here for college, but the reason I wanted to come here was because, to me, LA has always represented something bigger. I grew up in a small town in the Midwest, and I never really felt like I belonged there. I got picked on a lot because I wasn't skinny, or pretty, or interested in the things my classmates were. I was this awkward nerdy kid who always had my head in a book. I didn't fit in anywhere. My world felt so small, so gray."

Jade didn't talk about her past very often. But she still carried it with her, no matter where she went.

"Then, the summer before I started high school, we came to LA on vacation," she said. "And all of a sudden, everything was in color for the first time. It was like my whole world opened up. There were so many people, all different, all unique. I felt like I could be myself here, just one of millions of people living their lives their own way. So I worked my butt off all through high school, got into college on a full-ride scholarship, and moved here to chase my dreams."

"And what dreams are you chasing?" Simone asked.

"Nothing big. I never wanted to be an actor or a star like everyone else who comes to LA. I just wanted a different life for myself. To go to college, to build a career, to experience the world. I know those probably seem like small dreams, but I was the first person in my family to go to college. Just making it out of my hometown felt like a big achievement to me."

Simone squeezed Jade's arm gently. "I don't think your dreams are small. How does it feel to have achieved them?"

"Honestly, I don't know if I have. I don't think the life I dreamed of even exists. LA isn't perfect. It might look that way from the outside, but it's all superficial. I know that now, but when I first came here, it was like the city was full of potential. Like *life* was full of potential."

But that was a feeling she'd never get back. And it was a feeling Jade didn't *want* back. Because that naïve, optimistic outlook of hers had led to her getting her heart shattered.

Simone stroked her fingers through Jade's hair. "Don't give up on those dreams of yours just yet," she said. "You say you want to make something of yourself, but you already have. You're an exceptional woman, Jade."

Jade's stomach fluttered. Lying in Simone's arms, talking about her life, her dreams, felt natural. Comfortable.

Were they crossing a line into something beyond just physical? Was she letting her guard down, letting Simone in, in a way she'd told herself she wouldn't?

Was she setting herself up to have her heart broken all over again?

But when Simone leaned down and kissed her, none of that mattered.

Simone drew back, gazing into Jade's eyes. "Next Friday night," she said. "After the meeting with Ashton. After dinner, when our business is done. It will be just the two of us. And I think you're ready for me to take things to the next level."

Jade's heart skipped. "Do you mean…"

"I do," Simone said. "You're going to give me a *gift*."

That could only mean one thing. *Submission in its purest form. The most beautiful gift a submissive can give her Domme.*

The gift of herself. The gift of her trust.

Was Jade ready to give Simone that?

CHAPTER 17

"Here we are," Simone said. "The Ashton Star."

Jade stared out the car window as they pulled into the circular driveway at the front of the hotel. Above them, the old sandstone building towered eighteen stories high. With its elaborate facade, intricate stonework, and ornate pillars flanking the entrance, it resembled a palace more than a hotel.

Once the car had stopped, a valet wearing white gloves and a crisp suit opened the door for Jade. She stepped out onto the red carpeted walkway, gazing up at the building in awe.

"It's breathtaking, isn't it?" Simone said, joining her. "Just wait until you see inside."

Jade followed her boss through the front doors and into the lobby. Inside, the hotel looked even more like a palace, with sparkling crystal chandeliers and marble columns accented with gold. A stone fountain rose high in the middle of the lobby, the ceiling above them covered by a fresco of angels and cherubs cavorting among clouds.

And for the first time, Jade understood why Simone wanted so badly to make The Ashton Star hers. In a city known for ostentatious displays of glitz and glamour, the hotel possessed a sense of timeless luxury that was in a league of its own. It was the stuff of fantasies. But Jade was living that fantasy with Simone.

Her heart raced. It was mid-afternoon. There were only a few hours until their dinner with Ashton. And after dinner, it would be just the two of them, alone in the penthouse suite, the whole night ahead of them. And Jade would finally get to experience everything Simone had spoken of that evening on her couch.

It had only been a week since then, but it felt like so much longer. Every second she spent with Simone, she could feel the charge between them. And every moment they were apart, she could feel the distant pull of desire tugging in her chest.

Without warning, Simone seized Jade by the waist, pulling her into her body. Not a heartbeat later, a luggage cart pushed by a porter and stacked high with suitcases barreled past them, missing Jade by an inch.

"Careful now," Simone said. "I need you in one piece for tonight."

Jade let out a shaky breath. If Simone hadn't pulled her out of the way, she would have been knocked right over. But the cart had passed them now, and Simone still had her arms around Jade's waist in what was an entirely unprofessional embrace.

Keeping things professional between them was becoming harder and harder. Whenever they were alone in Simone's office, they weren't able to resist pushing the boundaries they'd set. A compliment or word of praise that carried the suggestion of something more. A firm command with a hint of playfulness, a reprimand that was little more than thinly veiled innuendo. A brief touch on the arm, the waist, the hip.

But never anything more. Never more than a flirtation. That line could never be crossed, no matter how blurry it was becoming.

"Ms. Weiss!"

Simone released Jade from her arms, turning toward the voice. A raven-haired man sporting a meticulously styled mustache and a sharp suit was hurrying toward them.

"I am so sorry." His voice carried a hint of a French accent. He turned to Jade. "Are you all right, Ms. Fisher?"

"Yes," she stammered.

"You have my sincerest apologies," he said. "I keep telling the porters to slow down, but they do not listen. I'll have a firm word with that one."

"It's all right," Simone said. "No one was hurt."

He offered her a polite nod. "Then allow me to introduce myself. I'm Jacques, the hotel manager. I wish to personally welcome you both to our hotel. If there is anything I can do to make your stay here more pleasant, please let me know."

Jade almost expected the man to bow to Simone. Had the staff been told to give them the VIP treatment?

"Thank you, Jacques," Simone said. "For now, we'd simply like to go up to our suite."

"I'll lead the way."

He guided them to the elevator, which had its own operator. But Jacques dismissed him, ushering Jade and Simone inside.

"Allow me." He pulled out a keycard, swiping it over the

elevator controls before pressing the button for the penthouse suite.

As the doors closed and they rode the elevator up to the
top floor, Jacques regaled them with the long and storied
history of The Ashton Star, oblivious to their lack of enthu-
siasm for the subject. They already knew everything there
was to know about the hotel. It made the ride in the old
elevator even slower than it already was.

Finally, they reached the top floor.

"Here we are," Jacques said, holding the doors open for
them. "The penthouse suite."

They stepped out of the elevator and into their suite.
And for the second time that day, Jade's breath was taken
away.

She gazed around the room, drinking it in. The high
ceilings, which made the vast suite feel even more spacious.
The polished floors, covered with ornate rugs and scattered
with plush vintage furniture. The tall windows, framed with
pure white curtains, overlooking the Los Angeles cityscape.
She could see for miles and miles.

It was no wonder Ashton had given them the penthouse
suite. It was designed to impress. And Jade was definitely
impressed.

"The main bedroom is through here," Jacques said,
leading them to a door and opening it up. Inside was a large
four-poster bed, covered in silk sheets and soft blankets. He
nodded in Jade's direction. "There's a pull-out bed for you,
Ms. Fisher. I'm assured it's quite comfortable, but if you'd
prefer your own room—"

"That's quite all right," Simone said. "I like to keep my
assistant *close*."

Heat rose to Jade's skin. She turned her head, looking

casually into the bedroom to hide the flush on her cheeks. Simone had to have known her words would elicit that reaction.

But Jacques didn't seem to notice. "Here are your room keys," he said, handing Simone two keycards. "I believe you have a reservation with Ms. Ashton for dinner at 8 p.m. downstairs. If you need anything before then, don't hesitate to reach out."

"Thank you, Jacques," Simone said.

The man took that as his cue to leave. With a polite farewell, he disappeared into the elevator.

Jade let out a breath. They were finally alone. Alone in this lavish hotel room, the silk-covered bed just a room away.

But Simone only gestured to the dining table, where a bottle of wine and a gift basket had been placed carefully next to a crystal vase filled with fresh flowers and a hand-written welcome card.

"Move all this," she said, "and set up my things on the table. We still have a few hours before we need to get ready for dinner, which gives us plenty of time to prepare. Go over that research file on Ashton and make sure you've memorized any talking points that are likely to come up."

Jade nodded. "Right away." There was always work to be done.

But her face must have betrayed her disappointment.

"Come here," Simone said.

Jade obeyed.

"I know you're looking forward to tonight, princess. Believe me when I say that I am too." Simone swept her gaze down Jade's body, amber eyes sparkling with lust. "I even bought you something to wear tonight. A dress for dinner. And a little something for afterward, for my eyes only."

Jade bit her lip. Did that mean what she thought it did?

"Here's what we'll do. You'll set up my laptop and we'll prepare. Then you'll put on that dress for me and we'll go down to the restaurant. We'll eat an exquisite meal, seal the deal with Ashton. And then," Simone whispered, leaning in close and drawing her thumb down Jade's cheek, "the night will be ours."

Jade's breath caught in her chest. Simone was close enough to kiss her, her soft, inviting lips barely an inch from Jade's own...

Simone drew back, pulling her hand away. "Let's get started, shall we?"

Jade sighed. It was going to be a long afternoon. And an even longer evening.

CHAPTER 18

S imone knocked on the bedroom door. "Are you ready? We need to get down to dinner."

"Almost!" Jade called. "Just give me a second."

A minute passed. Then the door opened and Jade stepped tentatively out of the bedroom. She'd undergone a transformation, her long hair pulled up into an elaborate bun, her pale blue eyes smoky and dark, her lips a subtle red. She wore an emerald-green cocktail dress with sequins that shimmered every time she moved and a low, scooped back that followed the lines of her curves, enhancing her voluptuous figure. The fitted dress ended above her knees, but the long sleeves kept it looking elegant rather than risqué. Yet there was a subtle flirtatiousness to it, just like Jade herself.

Simone had chosen well. Jade was stunning.

And tonight, she's all mine.

"There's just one more thing," Simone said. "One thing you're missing."

She beckoned Jade over to the dining table and picked

up a small, flat velvet box, opening it up before her. Inside was a white gold necklace adorned with diamonds and sapphires.

"A gift," Simone said. "From me to you."

Jade gazed into the box, the diamonds' sparkle reflected in her eyes. "It's beautiful. I couldn't possibly wear something like this."

"You can, and you will. Let me put it on for you."

Jade turned around. Simone took the necklace from the box and threaded it around Jade's neck, fastening it carefully. Then she stepped back and circled Jade slowly.

"Look at you." She skimmed her eyes down Jade's body and back up again. "Just look at you. How am I going to get through dinner with you sitting beside me looking so delectable?"

Jade lowered her eyes, avoiding Simone's gaze.

"You don't like the dress?" Simone asked.

"I do," Jade said quickly. "The dress, the necklace—I love them."

"Then what's the matter?"

"I'm just a little nervous. Don't get me wrong, I'm excited too, but all this is just…" Jade raised her hand to her neck, tracing her fingers over the necklace. "I feel like everyone is going to be staring at me."

"So let them," Simone said. "You're stunning."

Jade shook her head. "This is just a lot, that's all. The clothes, the five-star hotels, expensive dinners with executives and billionaires. I feel out of my depth, out of place. I feel like I don't belong."

Simone took Jade's cheek in her hand, fingertips caressing her skin. "You belong here, Jade. You do. You've worked for this. And not only the work you've done for me.

You've worked all your life to get to this moment. So *own it.* You're meant to be right here. You're meant to be at my side."

Simone drew her thumb down, tracing it along the curve of Jade's chin.

"Say it," she commanded. "Tell me where you belong."

"Here," Jade whispered. "With you."

Simone drew her in close, kissing her soft and slow. Jade melted into the kiss, her body yielding to Simone's. Desire rose inside her, urging her to hold Jade tighter, kiss her deeper, claim her there and then.

But business came first. And they couldn't afford to be late.

Simone pried herself away. "There's no one else I'd rather have by my side tonight. Let's get going."

They stepped into the elevator. As they rode it down to the restaurant, it took all of Simone's willpower to keep her hands to herself. *It would be the simplest thing to push her against the wall, kiss her, touch her, tease her, leaving her to sit through dinner all hot and bothered, waiting for the moment when I take her upstairs and do all kinds of wicked things to her...*

The elevator reached the third floor, where the hotel restaurant, an Italian fine dining venue, was located. Simone held the door open for Jade. But her assistant was no longer hesitant and unsteady on her heels like she had been up in the penthouse. Now she walked with the confidence of a seasoned executive on her way to a board meeting. The sight filled Simone with pride. And it made her want to bring Jade to her knees even more.

Business first. Pleasure later.

"Now," Simone said as they made their way to the

restaurant, "tell me about Ashton as if I know nothing about her."

"Well, her full name is Marissa Jean Ashton," Jade said. "She's in her 40s, born and bred in LA like every Ashton before her, although she went to college in New York State. She took over the family company in her 20s after her father died, which was when she started going by her surname, reasoning that the weight of her family name would help people take a young woman like her seriously in a male-dominated corporate landscape."

"Go on."

"Let's see, she's divorced, and has a daughter who isn't interested in the family business, so her nephew is next in line to take over. She's been restructuring the company in recent years, strategically selling off assets, streamlining their portfolio. Most of their hotels have been sold, but she's held onto The Ashton Star all this time."

"Until now."

"Until now," Jade echoed.

"Very good." They stopped at the entrance to the restaurant. "Are you wearing the rest of the gift I gave you?"

"You mean..." Jade's cheeks grew red. "Yes."

"I expect to see it after dinner. Now, pay attention in there. I'll be focused on working Ashton, so I need you as my second set of eyes and ears. Commit everything we speak about to memory. Make notes afterward if you need to."

Jade nodded, her usual determined expression returning. A moment later, the maître d' approached, greeting them by name before leading them through the restaurant to a small, private room at the back, where a table was set for three.

The maître d' pulled out a chair for Jade, but hesitated

before Simone, who pulled out her own chair and took a seat.

He gave them a polite nod. "I'll let Ashton know you've arrived."

Barely a minute passed before Ashton appeared, dressed in a dark pantsuit and heels. Simone rose to her feet, extending a hand to her. At a glance, the woman didn't look any older than Simone, but her dark shoulder-length hair had a sprinkle of white, a striking contrast to her still youthful face.

Ashton clasped Simone's hand, shaking it firmly. "It's a pleasure to finally meet you, Ms. Weiss."

"Call me Simone," she said. "And likewise."

Ashton turned to Jade, looking her up and down. "And this lovely young woman must be your date."

"My assistant," Simone said. "Jade Fisher."

"Oh?" Ashton shook Jade's hand. "That's right, you did tell me you were bringing your assistant. I'm so used to my dinner guests bringing dates along that I simply assumed. My mistake."

That hardly seemed like a natural conclusion to come to. Simone preferred to keep her private life out of the public eye, so for Ashton to know that Simone was interested in women meant she'd done her research. Or perhaps she'd simply figured it out on her own. Given that Simone had her own suspicions about Ashton's leanings, it wouldn't be surprising. She and Jade would need to be more careful.

As they took their seats again, a waiter appeared, introducing himself and informing them that he would be taking care of them personally for the evening. Dinner that night was a seven-course affair, the dishes carefully curated by the chef and paired with matching wines. Ashton certainly knew how to take care of her guests.

Within minutes, a team of waiters arrived carrying the first course, bruschetta accompanied by an apéritif, a dry white wine. Simone sipped hers slowly, and Jade did the same, having been warned by Simone not to overindulge in the wine. This was a business meeting, after all. They needed to keep their heads clear throughout the entire dinner.

And for what was to come afterward.

Simone turned to Ashton. "I'd like to thank you for your hospitality tonight. For providing us the opportunity to experience The Ashton Star for ourselves. It's an impressive hotel."

"You're quite welcome," Ashton said. "But we can skip the pleasantries. It's clear you're a woman who likes to get straight to business."

"I won't deny that. We both know what we want. We know what we're here for. So why waste time?" Simone set her glass down. "I want to buy your hotel. And you want to sell it to me."

"Is that so?" Ashton took a sip of her wine. "I do want to sell my hotel. But why would I want to sell it to *you?*"

"It's simple. You're going to sell me The Ashton Star because I'm going to restore it to its former glory. But you already know that." Simone leaned back in her chair, folding her arms across her chest. "You've seen my proposal and the plans for the redesign. At least, your nephew and the rest of your team have. But I know you wouldn't entertain a meeting like this without knowing exactly who and what you're dealing with, down to the last detail."

Even down to who the buyer likes in bed. Simone glanced at

Jade, who sat silently taking small bites of her bruschetta, no doubt committing every word of the conversation to memory. In the dress Simone had gifted her, the sapphire and diamond necklace around her pale, bare neck, she was just as distracting as Simone had predicted. Already, she was fighting off thoughts of ripping that dress off her assistant's body, and dinner had only just begun.

Perhaps having a little fun with her would make the time pass more quickly.

"You're right," Ashton said. "But I want to hear it from you. Tell me why I should sell my family's hotel to you."

"I'd ask the same question in your shoes," Simone said. "So I'll get straight to the point."

Underneath the table, she slid her foot out until it touched Jade's. Jade tensed, her eyes flicking toward Simone.

Slipping her foot out of her high heel, she drew it up the outside of Jade's leg. "Sell me this hotel," she said, "and I'll restore it to what it used to be. A shining beacon in a city of dreams. A star brought down to earth."

She outlined her vision for the hotel, her eyes never leaving Ashton's. At the same time, she slipped her foot between Jade's legs, pushing them apart. Slowly, sensually, she slid the side of her foot up the inside of Jade's calf, all the way up to her knee.

Jade's breath hitched, her leg trembling. But Ashton didn't notice a thing.

"A restoration of this scale is ambitious," Simone continued. "But I have a world-class team of architects and designers working for me, all in-house. I believe my assistant has forwarded you examples of their work on our other hotels?"

Simone turned her gaze to Jade, sliding her foot up the inside of Jade's thigh underneath her dress, brushing her toes against the soft, delicate skin there.

A faint flush crept up Jade's cheeks. "Y-yes. And we just finished remodeling Hotel Belvale in Santa Monica. I can send you the photos if you'd like."

"Hotel Belvale was in dire need of a facelift," Ashton said. "I'm interested to see what you've done with it."

"It's undergone a complete redesign while maintaining the building's original charm," Simone said. "Which is exactly what we're going to do with The Ashton Star."

Underneath the table, she slid her foot higher up Jade's inner thigh until her toes grazed the lace of her panties. Jade sucked in a sharp breath, dropping her fork to the table with a clatter.

She grabbed her glass of water, taking a long sip to cover it up. Simone pulled her foot back. That would be enough to keep Jade on her toes for the rest of dinner.

"And so," Simone concluded, "my plan will ensure that the legacy of The Ashton Star will continue. I'll transform it from the ground up. I'll make it shine again. And I'll make sure it lives on for decades to come."

She let the silence settle over them, allowing time for Ashton to digest her words. But it was all theater. Simone had Ashton hooked from the moment they'd first spoken on that conference call. Tonight's dinner was just another step in the dance.

"A touching pitch," Ashton said. "And a compelling one."

It was then that the next course arrived, a black truffle risotto paired with a pinot noir. Once the waiter had set their plates in front of them and retreated to the shadows,

Ashton picked up her fork and took a bite, chewing thoughtfully.

Finally, she placed her fork down again. "I can't deny that I'm impressed with your vision. Not to mention your dedication to revitalizing the hotel. I believe we can come to an agreement."

"Glad to hear it," Simone replied.

"There will, of course, be conditions, which we'll need to discuss in detail. Starting with the name of the hotel. As you've said, The Ashton Star has a reputation. It's a Los Angeles institution. Which is why I'll only sell it to you if you're willing to keep the name."

"I intend to keep the name," Simone said. "But with one small change. I want to call it *The Star.*"

Ashton crossed her arms. "You want to remove my family's name?"

"With all due respect, revitalizing the hotel will require a rebrand. It wouldn't make sense to keep the Ashton name."

"I can see where you're coming from. And I don't blame you for not wanting someone else's name on your hotel. But this?" Ashton gestured around. "It's my family's legacy, just like you said. It represents our place in the city. Is it selfish of me to want to hold onto that? Perhaps, but I do."

"I understand," Simone said. "But your legacy will live on regardless. It will live on in this building, in every brick, every piece of stone. What's a name in all of that?"

Ashton sighed. "I'll give you one thing. You know how to make a persuasive argument." She folded her hands on the table in front of her. "I like you, Simone. I like the vision you have for the hotel. And it's clear you believe in it. So if this is important to you, I'm willing to put my ego aside. And I'll admit that The Star has a nice ring to it." She turned to Jade. "What do you think of the name? Honestly?"

Jade hesitated, still flustered from earlier. But she managed to pull herself together. "I like it. It's simple but memorable. It suits a hotel as grand as this."

"All right," Ashton said. "Call it The Star. Just 'The Star' and nothing else. That's all I'll concede. The name needs to keep that connection to the hotel's history."

Simone nodded. "The Star it is."

The rest of dinner passed quickly, small talk mixed in with discussion of the finer details of Simone's plans for the hotel. As they finished dessert, the head waiter reappeared with a bottle of champagne, popping the cork and pouring them each a glass before retreating to the side.

Simone raised her champagne flute in the air before her. "To The Star."

Jade and Ashton echoed her words, drinking to the toast. It didn't take long before their glasses were empty.

As the waiter refilled them, Ashton excused herself to the bathroom. Soon, Simone and Jade were left alone, the waiter standing by unobtrusively at the side of the room.

Jade glanced in his direction, then back at Simone. "So that's it?" she said quietly. "The deal is done?"

Simone nodded. "Of course, there are contracts to exchange, details to iron out. Nothing is final until the papers are signed. But the hotel is as good as ours." She placed her hand on Jade's thigh under the table. "How does it feel to close your first deal?"

Jade shook her head. "I had nothing to do with it. I just sat here. You didn't need me at all."

"That's where you're wrong, Jade. You were the key to getting rid of the competition. You did all the grunt work behind the scenes. You're more than my assistant. You're my right-hand woman. I couldn't have done this without you by my side."

She leaned over and kissed Jade softly. The waiter was mere feet away, but Simone didn't care. At that moment, all she wanted was to kiss her sweet princess. And the way Jade trembled at the touch of her lips stirred an insatiable craving inside her.

Simone broke away. "Since we're done with business, why don't you go back up to our suite? I'll stay here and have one last drink with Ashton. That will give you time to prepare for the rest of the night." She slid her hand up the front of Jade's thigh. "I'll be up in an hour. And I expect to find you in the bedroom, on your knees, waiting for me. Lose the dress, but keep the necklace on. And let your hair down."

Jade nodded, her cheeks flushing pink. "Whatever you want."

"Now, hurry up and get out of here before I have to explain to Ashton why you're blushing like that."

Simone watched her leave, satisfaction and desire rippling through her. Jade was well and truly hers. Hers to command. Hers to claim. Hers to entrust with every part of herself.

And tonight, Simone would show her that.

CHAPTER 19

At the foot of the bed, in the penthouse suite of The Ashton Star, Jade waited.

On her knees. Her hair loose, gathered over one shoulder. The emerald-green dress hung carefully in the closet, leaving her dressed in the lingerie Simone had gifted her—a bra and panties made of the finest silk, black overlaid with lace as white and delicate as snow.

And Simone's necklace of diamonds and sapphires encircling her neck.

Jade's body pulsed with anticipation. What would Simone do when she walked through the door to find Jade waiting for her, on her knees, dressed in nothing but her gifts? Would she take Jade in with those mesmerizing amber eyes before devouring her with ravenous lips and hands? Would she tie Jade up and assail her with sensual delights while leaving her powerless to do anything but beg for release?

Would Simone make love to her in a way that was sweet and tender, but demanding and possessive at the same time?

The gift of surrender. That was what Simone wanted from her. That was what Jade longed to give her. Trust and vulnerability didn't come easy to her. But with Simone, it felt *right*.

The faint sound of the elevator arriving at the penthouse reached her, followed by the click of heels echoing up to the high ceilings as Simone made her way to the bedroom. Jade's heartbeat quickened. The last hour had crawled by. But now that the moment she'd been waiting for had arrived, the doubts in her mind reemerged. Was she truly ready for this? Would she ever be?

But she barely had a moment to second guess herself before Simone appeared in the doorway to the bedroom.

Jade peered up at her. She was still wearing the long mauve cocktail dress she'd worn to dinner, her hair in a loose updo and her lips an irresistible shade of red. Yet here and now, alone in their suite together, she was even more captivating than before.

Simone stepped into the room, hips swaying. "What a beautiful sight to come back to."

She circled around Jade, piercing eyes scorching her skin. Jade's breath deepened. She didn't move an inch.

"You have no idea how long I've waited for this moment," Simone said, sweeping her fingers along the back of Jade's shoulders. "To have you on your knees. At my feet."

She moved to stand in front of Jade, skimming her fingertips up Jade's neck, grazing the necklace around it.

"This will be just as sweet for me as it will be for you."

Jade quivered, electricity sparking through her at Simone's touch. She kept her head down, not daring to look her in the eye.

"Wait right here for me," Simone said. "Do not move. Do not speak. Wait. Understand?"

Jade nodded.

Simone's footsteps receded. Seconds passed in silence, then minutes. All the while, Jade waited for Simone for the second time that night.

And after an eternity, Simone returned to the bedroom. From Jade's place at the foot of the bed, her eyes downcast, all she could see of Simone were heeled feet and long legs clad in sheer black pantyhose pacing around the bedroom. As Simone stopped beside the bed, it took all Jade's willpower not to turn around.

Finally, Simone returned to stand before her. "You've done well to wait for me, kneeling in place so obediently all this time. But your Mistress is here now."

She leaned down, the scent of leather filling Jade's head as a long whip with dozens of tails fell into view. A flogger made of black suede, the handle intricately woven with silver threads.

Simone drew the handle up the center of Jade's neck, tipping her chin up. "Eyes on me."

Heart racing, Jade looked up at Simone. Her long blonde hair had been freed from its updo, cascading down her shoulders in waves. Gone was the mauve dress, replaced by a set of black lingerie dark as night and so sheer it was barely there, the bra revealing the faint outlines of two perfect nipples. A garter belt around her waist held up black thigh-high stockings topped with lace, and her feet were adorned in black heels.

"On your knees," Simone said. "At my feet. This is your place, always. Whether you're alone with me. Whether we're in the office, working side by side. Whether you're at home all by yourself late at night. Remember this. Remember where you belong."

Jade trembled, hypnotized by Simone's words, her voice. But nothing was as enthralling as the desire in her eyes, burning low and strong.

"Say it," Simone commanded. "Tell me where you belong."

"At your feet," Jade whispered. "I'm yours."

Simone trailed her fingers up Jade's throat and leaned down to kiss her. Jade shivered, her lips parting obediently, yielding to her. Simone's tongue danced against hers, soft but demanding, her breath whispering through Jade's body.

But only for the briefest of moments. Only for long enough to make her ache in her chest and between her thighs.

Simone straightened up, the flogger in her hand. "On your feet."

Jade rose to her feet, her stiff legs tingling. But she barely felt a thing. She was so entranced by the woman before her, so consumed by her need to obey her, serve her.

And Simone's next command sent a thrill through her.

"Get onto the bed."

Jade climbed onto the vast bed. As she lay down on her back, she noticed something atop the sheets beside her. A coil of rope. No, *two*.

Her heart began to pound. Ropes. A flogger. The same tools Simone had said were nothing more than props. But they were tools she wielded with an expert hand. And Jade longed to experience Simone's mastery of them.

"Soon, princess," Simone said, reading her mind. "First, this needs to come off."

Simone set the flogger on the bed, then leaned over and

reached around Jade's back, unclipping her bra. Jade sat up, allowing Simone to draw the straps from her shoulders, freeing her breasts.

Simone tossed the bra aside, her eyes skimming Jade's body. Other than her panties and the necklace around her neck, she was completely naked. And the hunger in Simone's gaze, as if she were moments from devouring her, made her feel even more exposed.

Simone picked up a coil of rope. "Hands and feet together.

Jade obeyed. Simone took the rope and bound Jade's wrists together, leaving a long tail trailing from them. Taking the other piece of rope, she moved down the bed to Jade's ankles, tying them together just like her hands.

Jade tested her bonds, pulling at her wrists and ankles. The ropes didn't budge. And with her arms and legs bound tight, she could barely move.

But Simone wasn't done. "Lie on your stomach."

Jade rolled over, tilting her head to watch as Simone tied her bound wrists to the headboard. Then she did the same to Jade's ankles, tying them to the foot of the bed, leaving her stretched out along the mattress, unable to do anything but squirm about helplessly.

Beside her, Simone picked up the flogger and drew it up the soles of Jade's feet, her calves, all the way up to her thighs.

"You look almost as good trussed up on the bed for me as you did at my feet. How does it feel to be bound and laid out for my pleasure?" She leaned down, her breath tickling the back of Jade's neck. "How does it feel to be mine for the taking?"

Jade quivered, adrenaline and desire surging through her. "Better than I ever dreamed."

A satisfied murmur rose from Simone. "Every moment we're together, every minute of every day, I've imagined all the ways I can make you mine. All the exquisite things I can make you feel. Pleasure. Pain. The ecstasy that comes with it."

She slid the flogger up to the top of Jade's thighs, letting its tails slip between her legs. Jade let out a sharp breath, the ache between her thighs deepening.

"You've already gotten a taste of the way pleasure and pain can mix and mingle, creating the most heavenly sensations," Simone said. "But pain isn't only a tool to enhance pleasure. Pain, all on its own, can be a release, freeing you from all your worldly worries, all your anxieties, all the thoughts and troubles in your mind." She traced her fingertips over the curve of Jade's hip, sending a shiver through her. "It grounds you in the present, forcing you to focus on the here and now. And in that space, where nothing exists but you and your Mistress? You're transported to a place that's more blissful than anything you've ever experienced."

"Subspace," Jade whispered. She'd read about it while looking up all the new words she'd learned from the questionnaire.

"That's right. And in that blissful space, where nothing exists but you and me? I become your only lifeline. It's a vulnerable state, and it requires you to trust your Mistress completely. So my question is, will you entrust yourself to me tonight? Will you give yourself to me, body, mind, soul? Will you have faith that I will keep you safe?"

"Yes," Jade said softly.

"Then close your eyes."

Jade hesitated. Being restrained was one thing. But not being able to see what was coming? The uncertainty, the complete loss of control? That was terrifying. It was why blindfolds were one of her hard limits.

But this wasn't anything like being blindfolded. She could open her eyes if she wanted to. And she had her safe words. *Red, yellow, green.* She still had her power.

And Simone would keep her safe.

Taking a deep breath, she shut her eyes.

Simone brushed her fingertips along Jade's arm. "Good girl."

And just like that, any doubts that remained were silenced. This was the side of Simone that had drawn Jade to her in the first place. The side that was as tender as it was firm, as gentle as it was commanding. The side of her she'd seen that first night in Simone's mansion when she brought Jade home and ordered her to rest while she took care of everything.

That side of her? It made Jade's heart flutter just as much as it made her body throb.

Slowly, Simone reached down to Jade's hips, taking the waistband of her panties and drawing them down to her bound ankles.

"Stay nice and relaxed like this," she said. "Don't tense up or try to anticipate me. And I'll be keeping an eye on you to make sure you're all right, understand?"

Jade nodded, burying her head in the pillow beneath her. Seconds passed, the rush of her pulse in her ears the only sound she could hear.

And when Simone brought the flogger down across Jade's ass, it was with a thud that reverberated through her whole body.

Jade winced. It had hardly hurt at all. But Simone liked to start slow, teasing her, tormenting her, building to a divine crescendo.

Would the climax be as earth-shattering as Jade had imagined?

Another firm thud as the flogger's tails fell upon Jade's ass. The next strikes were to her upper thighs, one after the other. More followed, in a practiced rhythm that echoed through the room, unceasing, unrelenting, each beat more intense than the last.

Jade hissed through her teeth, her arms and legs pulling against the ropes binding her to the bed. Her ass and thighs burned, each of the flogger's tiny tails a sharp sting on her raw, sensitized skin. But as the stinging subsided, it left behind a heat that set her body alight.

The flogger disappeared, replaced by the soft caress of Simone's hands.

"Did that hurt, princess?" she crooned.

Jade nodded.

"Do you want me to stop?"

Jade shook her head, her words muffled by the pillow. "Don't stop. Green."

"You're starting to feel it now, aren't you? How freeing this can be?"

Jade murmured wordlessly, drunk on adrenaline and sensation.

"Lean into that feeling," Simone said. "Surrender to it."

She brought the flogger down again, over and over, an unending melody of strikes that made Jade's body sing. The ropes around her wrists and ankles crumbled away. The bed crumbled away. Her inhibitions crumbled away. All that was left was the desire blazing through her body.

And when the next strike hit, Jade couldn't stop herself from crying out. Not in pain, but from an intense physical craving, a need for something she couldn't put into words.

No, it wasn't *something*. It was *someone*, Simone. Her touch. Her kiss. Simone's body against hers, her fingers inside her until she was utterly consumed by all that Simone was.

A desperate whimper rose from Jade's chest.

"I'm here." Simone placed her hand on Jade's shoulder. "Open your eyes. I'm right here."

Jade opened her eyes, blinking against the dim light. Simone was looking down at her, amber eyes shimmering, a soft smile on her lips.

Simone slipped into the bed beside her. "Let me look at you."

She nudged Jade gently onto her back. It was then that Jade realized while her wrists were still tied to the bed, her legs had been freed. Lost in an ocean of calm, she hadn't noticed Simone untie them.

And that wasn't the only thing that had changed. The lingerie Simone was wearing? All that was left of it was the garter belt and thigh-high stockings. Her bra and panties were gone, her body bared before Jade's eyes. Her perfect breasts, pale and round and luscious. Her pebbled nipples, an enticing pinkish brown. Generous thighs that framed the mound between her legs, which was covered in fine, neatly trimmed hair a shade darker than the hair on her head.

Jade had never seen anything more beautiful. And she'd never needed Simone more.

"You did so well," Simone said, drawing a hand down the side of Jade's face. "How do you feel?"

"Like I…" Jade's voice was barely a whisper. "Like I want you so bad it hurts."

Simone took Jade's face in her hands. "That's how I feel every time I look at you."

She brought her lips to Jade's, kissing her softly. Jade sighed into the kiss, arching against her. She could feel Simone's breasts pushing back against hers, could feel the heat of Simone's body on her skin, could taste the need on her lips. It only made Jade hunger for more.

Without breaking the kiss, Simone straddled Jade's body, gliding her hand down her neck, her breast, skating her fingertip over a pebbled nipple. Jade trembled, Simone's touch sending electricity coursing through her.

"Simone," she said, a plea and a prayer. "Oh, Simone…"

But she wouldn't be rushed. Her fingers still teasing Jade's nipple, Simone drew her lips down Jade's breast and took her other nipple in her mouth, sucking and flicking with her tongue. Jade writhed on the bed, straining at her bonds. She was so delirious with desire, so overcome with sensation. She couldn't contain herself any longer.

"Simone," she begged. "I need you. I *need* you."

Simone's breath deepened. She pushed Jade's legs apart and slipped between them, trailing her lips down the center of her stomach, lower and lower, until she reached the peak of Jade's thighs. Jade quivered, the throbbing in her core almost too much to bear.

"Please," she said softly. "Please…"

Simone ran her hands up the insides of Jade's thighs, spreading them even wider. Then she dipped down and parted Jade's lower lips with her tongue, sliding it up and down her folds in long, slow strokes.

Jade moaned, her head falling back, her hips rising from

the bed to grind against Simone's mouth. Her grip on Jade's thighs tightened, fingers digging into flesh as she worked her mouth faster, running her tongue over Jade's entrance, dipping and swirling, before dragging up to her swollen clit.

Jade gasped, her whole body shuddering. She was so sensitive! It only took a few sweeps of Simone's tongue and lips until she was right at the edge.

"Oh! *Oh!*"

She cried out as pleasure ignited inside her, rippling through her whole body. She arched into Simone, pulling at the ropes above her as her climax washed over her, threatening to toss her off the bed. And when it receded, it left a haze of bliss behind, clouding Jade's mind and body.

She sank back down to the bed, breathing hard. Somehow, the thirst inside her had only grown. Her need for Simone was insatiable.

So when Simone crawled up to kiss her, Jade channeled all her need into her lips, her body rising from the bed to press against Simone's. Simone purred into Jade's lips, pushing her back down to the bed, her eyes afire.

"I want you," she whispered. "I want you to come again. This time, with me."

She reached up and untied Jade's wrists. Setting the rope down on the nightstand, she picked something else up from it.

A strap-on. But it was the kind without straps, the kind that went inside the wearer too.

Simone pushed Jade's knees apart again, slipping between them to slide the short end of the strap-on inside Jade. She let out a hard breath. She was already so wet that it slid in easily.

Simone pushed Jade's legs back together and mounted

her hips, positioning herself above the strap-on jutting out from between Jade's thighs. "I want to watch you come undone," she said. "I want you to come undone with me."

Jade watched, enthralled, as Simone lowered herself down, burying the strap-on deep inside her. And slowly, she began moving her hips, up and down, back and forth. Jade gasped. She could feel Simone moving inside her, every motion sending pleasure darting through her.

And through Simone. With every movement, Simone trembled on top of her, her tremors reverberating through Jade's body. As Simone rolled her hips faster, Jade rocked her own hips in time, matching her rhythm, stoking the fire in Simone's core along with her own. She drew her hands up Simone's thighs, her hips, her waist, savoring the softness of her flesh. And when she slid them up to Simone's breasts, fingertips skating over her nipples, Simone murmured and moaned, her thighs clenching around Jade's hips.

"Yes," she said. "Touch me. Kiss me. Lose yourself in me."

She dipped down, her lips colliding with Jade's. Skin against skin, bodies pressed together, their tongues intertwined, their hands and fingers grasping, roaming, exploring. And as the pleasure inside them built and built, Simone's movements became more fevered, more frantic.

"Yes. Yes…" Simone's lips traveled up the side of Jade's neck to speak into her ear. "Come with me."

At her Mistress's command, Jade's body obeyed. She cried out, ecstasy surging through her. At the same time, Simone stiffened on top of her, her body quaking. Grinding and thrusting, kissing and caressing, they rode a wave of pleasure that carried them into the sweetest oblivion.

And even as they fell back down to earth, Jade remained

floating in a sea of bliss, safe in Simone's embrace. Simone, her Mistress. Simone, her lifeline. Simone, her everything.

This was the freedom granted by surrender, this euphoria, this release she shared with Simone. And despite it all, she found herself wanting more than this.

Despite it all, she found herself wanting to give Simone not just her body, but her heart.

CHAPTER 20

J ade burrowed deeper into the covers, her eyes closed, her head resting on Simone's shoulder. Simone lay in silence, feeling the gentle rise and fall of Jade's chest against her own, the tickle of her hair against her neck, the only sounds the whisper of Jade's breath and the distant noises of the city at night.

Her city, which stretched out beyond the penthouse windows, a sea of twinkling stars. And as of tonight, the most precious star in the city, The Ashton Star, was all but hers. Everything she'd worked for, everything she'd spent her career striving for, was within her grasp.

But it paled in comparison to the woman she held in her arms.

Jade stirred, her eyes fluttering open.

"You've come back to me," Simone said.

Jade gave her a lazy smile. "That was amazing. I *feel* amazing."

"You won't feel amazing tomorrow morning if I don't

get you something to drink. Sub drop can be worse than a hangover."

Jade traced a finger up Simone's arm. "Can't we lie here just a little longer?"

"All right," Simone said. "A little longer."

Jade let out a satisfied sigh, snuggling into Simone's body once again. "This was the best night I've had in a long time. Maybe even the best night of my life. I was so nervous about tonight. I've said it before, but I don't have a lot of experience with this kind of thing. I've only ever been with one other person and that… ended badly."

Jade trailed off, her eyes drifting to the window beside the bed.

"I guess what I'm trying to say is, I've never really had the chance to explore my sexuality. I was a bit of a late bloomer. I was never interested in guys, but I didn't even figure out I was gay until grad school. I never had much of a social life, let alone a romantic life or a sex life. I've just always been so focused on other things. Getting into college. Leaving my hometown. Grad school. That meant I missed out on a lot of the things you're supposed to do when you're young. And there have been so many moments where I've wondered if all the sacrifices I made were worth it." She looked up at Simone, her eyes shimmering. "But right here? Right now? For the first time, it all feels worth it."

Simone drew a hand down Jade's arm. "You know, I see so much of myself in you. I grew up here in LA, but I had a rough childhood. My family didn't have much, and after my parents got divorced, things became even more difficult. My father refused to pay child support, and my mother struggled to put food on the table, struggled to keep a roof over our heads. It was hard. So I made it my goal to escape that life, pouring everything into my studies, and eventually my career."

"I didn't know that about you," Jade said. "When I applied for this job, I read every interview you've ever done. You never spoke about your upbringing in any of them."

Simone stretched out on her back, staring up at the ceiling. "It can be difficult to talk about. A lot of it wasn't pretty. My parents' divorce was messy, to say the least. I became nothing but a pawn for them to use against each other. Half of my childhood was spent being pulled between them, ripped from one home to another, with no sense of security."

"That sounds awful."

"You don't know the half of it. A year or so after the divorce, my mother picked me up from school and told me we were going on a vacation. That 'vacation' involved us hiding out in a hotel room on the other side of the country. After three weeks, the police came knocking at the door. They arrested my mother, dragged me into a police car, and told me I'd been kidnapped. I would have been nine or so, far too young to understand what was going on. Being thrown in the back of a police car in the middle of the night was much more traumatizing than my mother taking me away was."

"I'm so sorry you went through that," Jade said. "Why did your mom do it?"

"As far as I've ever been able to tell, it was simply out of spite. She hated my father, and he gave her plenty of reasons to. The entire time they were together, he was cheating on her with half a dozen other women. And when she found out, it broke her."

Her mother was never the same after that. And after the divorce, she'd turned to alcohol. Every night, she'd get drunk and rant and rave to Simone about her cheating bastard of a father.

Don't ever get married, she would say. *Don't ever rely on any man.*

Love is bullshit. It makes you weak. You need to be strong, baby.

You can't trust anyone. They'll just betray you in the end.

"The resentment she harbored for my father was far stronger than her love for me," Simone said. "Everything she did—everything they both did—was to hurt each other. They didn't care what I wanted, what I needed. Eventually, I learned that I needed to look out for myself because no one else would."

And when she turned eighteen and left home, neither of her parents made any attempt to stay in contact with her. Her mother lost herself in a bottle, drowning out her misery and resentment over her broken marriage. Her father simply disappeared.

Jade placed her hand on Simone's chest. "That's horrible. You were just a kid. You deserved better."

"Perhaps. But everything I went through made me who I am. It made me determined that my life would be different. I resolved that I would never have to depend on anyone else, that I'd always have a stable home, the security I was missing as a child. I would build a life for myself, one that no one could tear away from me. And I've done that. It's taken hard work, sacrifice, but I've done it."

"And you think it's all been worth it?" Jade asked.

"I do." Simone turned to face Jade again. "Because it led to this singular moment. It led me to you."

As she swept Jade into her arms again, a familiar voice rang out in the back of her mind.

Love makes you weak. You need to be strong.

Simone would allow herself to be weak for one night, no longer. Because what was between them could never be anything but a carnal affair.

Even if a part of her wanted something more.

CHAPTER 21

"Good morning." Jade placed a cardboard tray holding two cups of coffee on Simone's desk, taking one from it and sliding it towards her. "Here's your coffee."

Simone murmured a hello and picked up the coffee cup, her eyes not leaving her screen. Jade took a sip of her own coffee, tossing the cardboard tray in the recycling.

"Would you like to hear what's on the schedule for today?" she asked.

"Go ahead," Simone said.

"You have a call with the investors from New York at ten. You have lunch with Olivia De Leon to discuss her upcoming trip. And legal wants to meet with you next week to finalize the revisions to The Ashton Star contract."

"Tell them we'll meet on Tuesday. That will give me time to go over the changes."

"Sure thing. And it's Maxine from reception's birthday. I ordered some flowers for her from you."

"Good. One more thing." Simone finally looked up at her. "Come here."

Jade rounded the desk. Simone swiveled her chair around to face her, plucking the coffee from her hand and setting it down on her desk. Then she took Jade's hands and pulled her onto her lap, smothering her gasp of surprise with a fiery kiss.

Jade murmured into her lips, heat rising inside her. She drew her hands down Simone's chest, pushing back against her playfully.

"I thought we weren't supposed to do this at work," she said.

"Shut up and let me kiss you." Simone pressed her lips to Jade's again. "I couldn't resist with you looking like that."

So Simone had noticed her new outfit? Now that she had a steady paycheck, she'd decided to treat herself to some new clothes. She'd all but given up on finding nice clothes that flattered her figure, but the designer outfits Simone bought her had inspired her.

And while her new clothes weren't designer, they were far more stylish than the outfits she normally wore to work, not to mention more daring. Today, she wore a short, royal blue sheath dress and black heels that were both fashionable and comfortable enough to wear all day. Her hair was loose, but styled in a way that kept it out of her face, and she'd added a touch of lipstick. Even Jade had to admit that she looked hot.

"What's even sexier than that dress is the way you wear it," Simone said. "I don't know how I'm going to get anything done today when all I'll be thinking about is the hundred different ways I could fuck you right here in my office."

"Are you saying that just to make me blush?" Jade murmured.

"It's working, isn't it? And while I do love to make you blush, I'm saying it because I mean it."

Jade's cheeks burned even hotter. Ever since that night in the penthouse, Simone had all but given up on keeping everything between them professional at work. Sure, when others were around, they maintained the facade of being nothing more than boss and assistant. But when they were alone, they were barely able to keep their hands off each other.

"I'm certainly going to miss this when my old assistant gets back," Simone said. "For all her wonderful qualities, you're much better at serving me in the ways that really matter."

Jade felt a pang of yearning in her stomach. She'd been trying not to think about the fact that her time as Simone's assistant would end in less than a month. What would happen then? Would they still get to see each other?

Would their kinky affair come to an end?

"Jade?" Simone said. "What's the matter?"

Jade shook her head. "It's nothing. I'm going to miss this too, that's all."

Simone took her hand, lacing her fingers through Jade's. "Just think about it this way. Once you're no longer working for me, we won't have to sneak around. Doesn't that sound appealing?"

Jade's heart skipped. So Simone did want to keep seeing her.

And maybe? Maybe it could even be more than just an affair.

Jade smiled. "That sounds great."

Simone released Jade's hand. "Now, we have plenty to do, so get to your desk."

But the moment Jade got up from her lap, Simone pulled her back into a hungry kiss. And when her boss finally released her, it was with a sharp slap on her ass that made her hot all over.

Jade sat down at her desk, coffee in hand. She really did have plenty of work to do. Both of them were still working overtime on the Ashton Star deal. While an agreement had been reached, there were minor details to negotiate, paperwork to finalize. Simone wouldn't rest until the contract was signed and the ink was dry. And neither would her assistant.

But for Jade, working with Simone was effortless. They worked together like one, both inside and outside the office. All Simone had to do was say the word, and Jade would be there to carry out her every command. Half the time, Simone didn't need to say anything at all. Jade knew exactly what her boss needed before she even had to ask.

And in return? Simone looked after Jade's needs in other ways. Buying her things, taking her home for dinner, making sure she had the occasional evening off. And every time Jade protested, she was met with a familiar line. *You're no use to me if you're dead on your feet.* For a woman notorious for being a harsh taskmistress, Simone sure was soft on her.

But Jade couldn't deny how good it made her feel. She hadn't realized she needed someone looking out for her until Simone started taking care of her. She hadn't realized how much she relished Simone's praise until Simone told her how brilliant she was.

She hadn't realized she needed Simone until she swept into her life and swept her off her feet.

And now, the two of them were irrevocably intertwined,

the connection between them stronger, deeper, than anything Jade had felt before.

She turned on her laptop. She couldn't afford to get lost in her thoughts when she had so much to do. As she waited for her laptop to boot up, she checked her inbox on her phone. She was waiting for an email from a recruiter about a new job. She hadn't started seriously applying for jobs yet. Three months of working for Simone would give her enough money and experience to take her time finding something new. But she'd put out a few feelers, just in case.

She scrolled through her inbox. It was mostly full of junk. But as she set her phone down on her desk, an unopened email caught her eye. It was the alumni newsletter from her grad school. The subject line?

Professor Philippa Roberts wins prestigious research prize.

Her stomach dropped. *It's her.* Jade couldn't even say her name, *think* her name, without it bringing everything to the surface. The anger. The betrayal. The heartbreak.

But that was all in the past where she'd buried it, steeling her heart against it, making herself strong enough for it not to get to her. She wasn't that naïve, fragile girl any longer. She wouldn't let her—let *Philippa*—get to her.

Her hand hovered above her phone screen. Just one swipe and the email would be gone. She would never have to think about Philippa again.

But as she scanned the subject line, a question nagged at her.

The research. What was it? Jade had to know.

She opened up the email and scrolled down. A photo of an auburn-haired woman filled Jade's screen, her perfect smile blinding. But Jade knew what was behind Philippa's smile. She knew what was behind those eyes.

And as she skimmed the paragraph beneath Philippa's photo, her fears were confirmed. The research? It was Jade's research project from her first year of grad school. The project she'd worked so hard on day after day, late into the night, with Philippa at her side, the forbidden tension between them threatening to boil over.

Until finally, it did. And then everything had fallen apart.

Jade closed her eyes and took a deep breath. She didn't want to think about *her* right now. Not when everything was going so well in her life. She needed to put it all behind her, where it belonged.

But how could she? How could she move past everything Philippa had done to her? It had been two years, but suddenly, it felt fresh and raw, as if it had only been yesterday—

"Jade?"

She glanced up from her phone and over to Simone's desk. Simone was looking back at her with narrowed eyes.

"Did you hear a word I said?" Simone asked.

"Uh, sorry," Jade said quietly. "I was distracted."

Simone's brows drew together. "Is everything all right?"

Jade nodded. "Everything's fine." She closed the email and set her phone on her desk, face down. "I was just reading some emails."

Simone didn't question her further, but her suspicion was clear in her eyes. Could she tell that Jade was lying?

But this wasn't something Jade could share with her. She'd never told a single soul what had happened between her and Philippa. Who could she trust with a secret so shameful?

Maybe she *could* trust Simone with her secret. Simone

understood her in a way that no one else ever had, cared for her in ways that no one else did.

But that was what Jade had thought about Philippa.

She shook her head. She was letting Philippa get to her. Simone wasn't like that. She wouldn't use Jade the way Philippa had. She wouldn't break Jade's trust.

She wouldn't shatter her heart like Philippa had.

CHAPTER 22

J ade pushed her food around on her plate. It was early in the evening, and they'd gone back to Simone's mansion after she insisted they leave the office for a change of scenery. She'd ordered them dinner, but Jade didn't have an appetite.

She put down her fork, eliciting an unimpressed look from Simone. "Aren't you going to eat anything?"

Jade shrugged. "I'm not hungry."

"Just like you weren't at lunchtime? Don't think I didn't notice you skipped your lunch break. I didn't say anything because you were clearly upset about something."

"I have a few things on my mind, that's all. But I can still get my job done."

"I didn't bring you back here to work, Jade. I brought you back here because I thought you needed a little down-time." Simone reached across the table and put her hand on Jade's. "And I thought we could spend some time together. We haven't had the chance to be alone outside the office since that night at The Ashton Star."

Jade glanced down at her plate. "I'm not really in the mood for that."

"*Not in the mood?* Do you think I want..." Simone pulled her hand back. "That's *not* what I meant. Not at all."

"Right." Jade shook her head. "I'm a little tired. If you don't need me tonight, I should just go home."

"Jade, wait. I'm worried about you. I know something is wrong. I don't know what it is, and you don't have to tell me, but I want to help."

"You can't help," Jade said. "Not with this."

"Perhaps, but let me try. Stay here with me tonight. Let me take care of you. It's not going to fix whatever is going on, but it might help you feel a little better."

Jade hesitated. No small part of her wanted to be alone, to curl up in her bed and let all the feelings she'd been holding back all day consume her.

But another part of her wanted someone by her side to tell her that everything was going to be okay.

"What do you say?" Simone asked. "Will you stay here tonight?"

Jade nodded. "I'll stay."

Simone got up from the table. "Wait right there while I prepare some things for you. And try to eat something."

Simone disappeared upstairs. Jade took a few bites of her dinner, chewing and swallowing mechanically before pushing the food around on her plate. She almost didn't notice when Simone returned.

"Everything is ready for you." She held out her hand. "Come."

Jade took Simone's hand and got to her feet. Simone led her up the stairs, into her bedroom, and into the ensuite bathroom. Inside, the jacuzzi tub was filled to the brim, a haze of steam hovering over it. Rose petals danced on the water's surface, their fragrance mixing with the vanilla-scented candles that sat on the rim of the bath. Nearby, a pile of bright white bath towels was folded carefully on a bench, and a soft, fluffy bathrobe hung by the door.

"If you'd like some space, I can leave," Simone said. "Will you be all right by yourself?"

"Yes, but…" Jade glanced up at her. "Can you stay?"

"Of course." She squeezed Jade's hand before releasing it. "Now, get undressed and get in before it gets cold."

Jade stripped off her clothes piece by piece, avoiding Simone's gaze. Simone had seen her naked before, so why did she suddenly feel so exposed?

She shielded her body with her arms as she hung up her clothes on a nearby hook, then stepped toward the bath.

"Wait," Simone said. "Your hair."

Jade brought her hand to her head. Her hair was loose and would get soaked as soon as she sat in the bath.

But Simone was already behind her, gathering her hair in her hands. Jade watched in the mirror as Simone wound it into a bun at the top of her head, securing it with a single hair tie.

"There." Simone swept her hand gently down the side of Jade's neck. "That's better."

A warm shiver radiated through her. She stepped into the bath and sank into the water, letting the gentle flow of the jets caress her body, the sweet floral scents enveloping her. The water was perfect, not too hot, not too cold. And something in it made it smooth and milky, like liquid silk.

Jade stole a glance at Simone. She'd taken a seat on the edge of the bath, her feet bare on the plush mat beside it. Her presence was comforting. But Jade wanted her closer.

"Will you get in with me?" she asked.

Simone gave her a soft smile. "Whatever you need."

Rising to her feet, she stripped off her dress, then her underwear. Jade averted her gaze. It felt wrong to look at Simone that way now. Jade wanted to be held by her, that was all.

But she didn't have to ask. Simone lowered herself into the tub at the other end, beckoning Jade to her. As Jade slipped between her legs, Simone wrapped her arms around her, pulling her close. Jade leaned back against her, sinking deeper into the water, a heavy sigh falling from her chest.

Simone kissed the side of Jade's head. "That's it. Just let go."

Jade closed her eyes. She let her body relax, let all the tension in it melt away. She stopped holding back, stopped holding it all in.

And she let go of everything.

A gentle sob rose through her body, then another, then another, tears spilling from her eyes. She pulled her knees up to her chest, wrapping her arms around them as she trembled in Simone's embrace.

"That's it," Simone said, her arms tightening around her. "Just let it all out."

Just like always, Jade couldn't help but obey. Her sobs grew louder, her tears flooding forth freely, tremors racking her whole body.

She didn't try to stop them. She let her sobs echo through the room, violent war cries against all the pain and hurt inside her. She let the tremors surge through her, purging all her dark thoughts from her body. She let her tears, her heartache, flow into the water beneath her until they dissolved into nothing.

And through it all, Simone held Jade's body to hers, riding each wave of emotion with her. "I've got you," she said softly. "I've got you."

Slowly, Jade's sobs turned into breaths. Her body calmed, her eyes dried. She had no tears left to cry. Nothing left inside her but the sweet freedom of release.

Seconds passed in silence, then minutes. Simone loosened her hold on her, but didn't let go. Jade relished the feeling of Simone's arms around her, the touch of her skin, the scent of her hair. It grounded her just like it had that night in the hotel.

"How are you feeling?" Simone asked.

"A little better," Jade said quietly. "That really helped."

"If you think talking will help too, I'm here to listen. Whenever you feel ready."

Jade swallowed. "I-I think I'm ready."

Simone picked up a loofah that was floating in the water and drew it gently down the back of Jade's arm. "Tell me what's been troubling you."

"Well, I..." Jade leaned back against her once again. "I got an email this morning. It was nothing, just a grad school newsletter. But it had an article about one of my professors in it. Except she wasn't just my professor."

How could Jade explain what had happened between them? She'd never told a single soul. She'd been carrying that shameful secret with her for two years.

Simone swept the loofah up Jade's arm, over her neck and shoulders, letting the water cascade down her chest and back. "Just take your time. Take all the time you need."

Jade drew in a deep, steadying breath. "Her name is Philippa. Well, Professor Roberts, but she always let us call her by her first name. From the beginning, it felt more like she was another student than a professor. She was barely 30, and she was pretty close to her students. There were rumors that she was a bit *too* close to some of them, but I figured that was just gossip. Everyone loved her."

That was why it had felt so easy to trust her. And that was why Jade had felt like she couldn't tell anyone about what happened between them.

"I ended up with her as my graduate adviser in my first year," she said. "She helped me a lot, and not just with my grad project. I was a little younger than everyone else in my class. I skipped a grade in elementary school, and after college, I went straight to grad school, so I was only twenty-one when I started. It was hard, trying to navigate everything. But Philippa was there for me."

Simone listened in silence, drawing the loofah up and down Jade's back, the soothing motions and the gentle embrace of the water lulling her into a state of calm.

"Over time, we became close," she said. "Closer than was normal for a student and a professor. I had a crush on her from the beginning, so when she started giving me all this attention, it was exciting. That crush was how I realized I liked women in the first place. So when she kissed me…"

Jade's voice quavered. She swallowed the lump in her throat. "When she kissed me, I didn't do anything to stop her. I wanted it. One thing led to another, and we ended up having sex. It happened again and again, until it became a relationship. At least, that was how I saw it. She kept us secret, but that was so we wouldn't get in trouble. Otherwise, she treated me like I was her girlfriend, inviting me back to her place, spending time with me like we were a couple. She was my first everything. My first kiss. My first love. I even lost my virginity to her."

Her stomach churned. She didn't dare turn around, didn't dare look Simone in the eye. Otherwise, she wouldn't be able to go on.

"Things were so good at first," she said. "But Philippa always reminded me that I needed to keep things between us secret. 'You wouldn't want anyone to find out about us, would you?' she would say. 'You wouldn't want me to lose my job.'

"At first, her words were just a warning to be careful. But then, they became threats, a way for her to control me. If I disagreed with her or did anything she didn't like, she'd remind me that I was breaking the rules by being with her. That if anyone found out about us, I'd get kicked out of grad school. Everyone would know what I did, and I'd be humiliated, my reputation, my whole life, ruined. So I needed to stay in line. I needed to do what she said." Jade shook her head. "I should have broken things off with her right there and then. But I didn't, because I was in love with her."

She braced herself for Simone's judgment. But she didn't say a word, didn't react at all. Instead, she continued drawing the loofah over Jade's breasts and stomach, massaging gently.

That was what Jade needed from her. To know that she was there. To know that she was listening.

"I was so in love with her that I was blind to the fact that how she treated me was wrong," Jade said. "And that she wasn't in love with me at all. The whole time, she was just using me. For sex. For other things. It was only after half the year went by that I realized it. And I only realized it because I was at her apartment one night and she'd left something on the table I wasn't meant to see. It was a research paper she'd submitted to a journal. And when I read the paper, I realized it was *my* research. She'd stolen my project."

At first, Jade had been confused, thinking it was some kind of mistake. How stupid she'd been.

"When I confronted her about it, she didn't deny it," Jade said. "She'd taken the data and my half-written paper from my laptop, tidied it up, and submitted it as her own work. She said she'd helped me with it, so it was justified. That was how it worked in academia, she said. But she didn't even put my name on it. I was stupid enough to believe her, but that didn't stop me from feeling betrayed. And when I told her how I felt, she blew up at me.

"She asked me what I was going to do about it. Tell someone? No one would believe a student over a professor. I'd be branded a troublemaker and kicked out of the grad program, so I'd better keep my mouth shut. And I'd better keep my mouth shut about our relationship, too. Because who would even believe me? Who would believe that Philippa would ever want *someone like me?*"

Something stabbed inside Jade's chest. Those words had cut her deep. She'd left all of that behind her long ago. The mean girls at school making jabs about her body. The loneliness of being ostracized. The feeling that she'd never be good enough. She'd fought her whole life to feel comfortable in her own skin, to be proud of the person she was. And Philippa had undone it all with just a few words.

"She said that if I tried to tell anyone about us, she'd make everyone think I was crazy. That I was some kind of stalker who was obsessed with her. That *she* was the victim, not me. Everyone would think I was a liar, a slut. She would make sure of it. I couldn't believe what I was hearing. I couldn't believe that she'd turned on me the way she had.

But…" Jade shook her head. "But the truth was, she'd always been that way. I was just in denial about it. But that night, there was no denying it. She didn't care about me. She only wanted me to be her obedient little sex doll. And after I stepped out of line, she didn't want me anymore. She kicked me to the curb like I was nothing."

Jade's voice faltered. Simone had her arms around her again, the loofah cast aside. Jade watched it float away, her vision blurry with tears she wouldn't let fall.

"That realization?" she said. "It broke me. I ended up flunking out of the semester and moving back to my hometown to live with my parents. They thought I burned out. After all, I'd left home so young, moving to the big city all by myself. It wasn't surprising that I couldn't handle it. I let my parents believe that. I let everyone believe that. Because I couldn't tell them the truth. Like Philippa said, who would believe me? Even if they did, what could anyone do about it?

"I spent the next few months at home, barely leaving my bedroom. But eventually, I left my room, then my house. Eventually, I started living my life again. And when the next semester started, I went back to grad school. I was assigned a new adviser, and I did my best to pretend Philippa didn't exist whenever I saw her. I finished my first year, and then the rest of the grad program. I moved on. But I never really got over what Philippa did. It changed me."

That innocent girl Jade had once been? That optimistic dreamer? She was long gone now.

"Sometimes, I think about what would happen if I could travel back in time and meet my younger self," she said. "Would she be horrified by how jaded and cynical I've become? Would she think there was something wrong with me? It's like Philippa broke something inside me, some light, some spark, that I can't ever get back. And it makes me feel like she won in the end. It's been two years and I still can't hear her name without falling apart. That email this morning brought everything back. Everything she did to me. All the ways she used me. And the humiliation, the shame I feel over letting her use me in the first place."

Jade fell silent, the faint swish of water the only sound in the room. And as sadness welled up inside her again, Simone spoke for the first time.

"Oh, Jade," she said. "None of that was your fault. Philippa took advantage of you. You can't blame yourself for that. And you have *nothing* to be ashamed of. She's the one who should be ashamed, preying on you the way she did."

"I know that," Jade said. "At least, I know that logically. But at the same time, I keep second-guessing myself. We were both adults. And I wanted it. She never forced me to be with her or anything like that."

But was that really true? When Jade thought about that time in her life, everything was so fuzzy. But she remembered the constant pressure, the feeling like she couldn't say or do anything Philippa didn't want her to do. She'd bulldozed over Jade's needs, shutting her down, not giving her any real choice but to do what *she* wanted.

And while Jade had been naïve, Philippa hadn't been. She had to have known what she was doing. She had to have known how impressionable Jade was. Had she used that to bend Jade to her will without Jade realizing it?

Simone interrupted her thoughts. "Even if she didn't force anything on you, that doesn't make what she did okay. Her actions, the way she treated you, were wrong."

"I know. I know that. But it's hard to accept it sometimes. Because what good does it do to admit that she took advantage of me? What am I supposed to do about that fact? Report her? She was right. It's hard enough to report this kind of thing when it's a male professor. When it's a woman? A woman *and* a female student? Who would believe that? All I'd end up doing is dredging up everything that I've spent the last two years trying to move on from."

"I understand," Simone said. "There's no right or wrong way to handle a situation as difficult as this, no right or wrong choice. What matters is that you choose the path that allows you to live your life. You've already made a brave choice in telling me all this tonight."

"You're the first person I've ever told. I've never even said out loud that what Philippa did to me was wrong."

"I know that couldn't have been easy for you. I'm proud of you."

"It was hard," Jade admitted. "But it helped."

"I'm glad. And if you ever need to talk some more, I'm here for you." Simone stroked Jade's arm gently. "I'm sorry Philippa did that to you. I'm sorry she made you feel broken. But I know you still have that spark inside you. I see it every time I look at you. I see it in your eyes when you smile. And I feel it whenever you talk about your dreams, about the future. So don't lose hope. Don't lose that part of yourself that yearns for something more. It's what makes you shine the way you do. And it would break my heart to see it disappear. So promise me you'll hang onto it."

Jade's stomach fluttered. "I will."

Simone took Jade's hands in hers, tracing her fingertips over the wrinkles on Jade's fingers. "We've been in here far too long. Let's get you dried off and into something warm."

Slipping out from behind her, Simone got up and drew

Jade out of the bath, wrapping her up in a soft white bath sheet before taking another towel and drying her body from head to toe. It wasn't until she'd dried Jade off completely and bundled her into a warm, fluffy bathrobe that Simone toweled herself dry and slipped into a robe of her own.

She led Jade back into the bedroom. "It's getting late. You should get some rest. You can sleep in here with me tonight."

Jade nodded. And as she slipped into the bed, all the doubts she'd had about Simone seemed foolish. She was nothing like Philippa. Simone cared about her, really cared. And if Jade was ever going to trust anyone with her heart again, it would be Simone.

But to do that? She needed to put everything with Philippa behind her.

Which meant she had a choice to make.

CHAPTER 23

Simone stood by her office window, looking out over the Los Angeles cityscape. It was late in the evening, and the sun was setting over the city.

She'd barely had a chance to enjoy the view when her phone rang.

Simone picked up the call. It was Olivia. "Back in town already?"

"My flight just landed," Olivia replied. "How has Club Velvet fared while I was away?"

"Just fine. The three of us took care of it."

"And the private rooms?"

"The finishing touches are done. The paperwork and insurance are sorted, and we're on track to open them next week. But I'm more interested in hearing about your trip." Olivia had gone to New York on business and had taken the opportunity to do some scouting and networking for Club Velvet, visiting half a dozen clubs like it on the East Coast. "Learn anything useful?"

"Not as much as I'd hoped," Olivia said. "We're one of the

few BDSM clubs in the country that caters exclusively to the sapphic market. Some have ladies-only events, but nothing like Club Velvet. One was owned by a lesbian couple we could learn a thing or two from. I believe you're already acquainted with Vanessa Harper? She and her wife own Lilith's Den."

"We've met once or twice on business," Simone said.

"She said as much. I told them to let me know next time they're in LA so we can all get together and trade ideas."

"I'll reach out to her, let her know they're welcome to come by at any time."

The click of heels interrupted her as Jade slipped back into the office, a bound document in her hand.

Simone held up a finger in Jade's direction, speaking to Olivia. "I'll let you get home. I'm looking forward to discussing your findings with you in more detail later."

"Likewise," Olivia said. "Talk soon."

As Simone hung up her phone, Jade joined her by the window. In the days since she'd spent the night at Simone's house, Jade had been quieter, more reserved. Simone had been giving her the space she needed, all the while fighting the urge to track Philippa down and ruin her the way she'd threatened to ruin Jade. It was what she deserved.

But the battle wasn't Simone's to fight. How Jade dealt with Philippa was her choice, and hers alone. The best Simone could do was be in Jade's corner.

"Here." Jade handed her the document. "The report you wanted. I've flagged all the important parts."

Simone flipped through it before setting it aside on the coffee table in front of the window. "Excellent work."

Jade's cheeks flushed. That was her usual reaction to praise, but it had been absent in recent days.

"You seem much better today," Simone said. "It's good to see you smile again."

"It's all because of you," Jade said. "When I got that email the other day, it was like I was dragged right back to when everything with Philippa went down, and I just fell apart. But you were there to catch me. I don't know what I would have done without you."

"All I did was listen."

Jade shook her head. "It was more than that. You listened without judging me. You let me pour my heart out to you. You were there when I really needed someone. And you've been there for me in so many ways."

She reached out and took Simone's hand, her gaze dropping to her feet.

"You always know the right thing to do, to say, to make me feel comfortable and confident. You've helped me realize things about myself, discover parts of myself that I didn't even know existed. You always give me exactly what I need, even when I don't know that I need it. And that?" She looked up at Simone, meeting her eyes again. "That means the world to me."

Simone cupped Jade's cheek in her hand. "*You* mean the world to me, Jade."

She leaned in and pressed her lips to Jade's. Jade deepened the kiss, igniting the embers within Simone's body. She could feel the same desire in Jade, in her lips, in the way her body pressed back against Simone's, in the thumping of her heart against Simone's chest.

Jade drew back slightly. "I've been thinking, and I want to repay you. You're always taking care of me, and I..." She peered up at Simone from under her eyelashes. "I want to take care of you, for once."

The heat inside Simone's body flared. The lust in Jade's eyes, the thirst in her voice—she wasn't hiding behind coy glances and murmured words any longer. This side of Jade, this confident, passionate side, had grown stronger over time, but after everything with Philippa reared its ugly head, it had all but disappeared.

Tonight, a glimpse of it was showing again. And Simone wanted nothing more than to draw it back out.

"I want to serve you," Jade said, her voice soft and honey-sweet. "Please, Mistress?"

Simone drew in a deep breath. This broke all of her rules, both written and unwritten. While they'd long dropped the pretense of keeping business separate from pleasure, this was the one line they hadn't crossed, the only remaining boundary between their personal and professional lives.

And they had an understanding. Simone held the reins. Simone decided when, and where, and how. Simone controlled every element of Jade's pleasure.

But Jade lived to fulfill her every whim. She lived for Simone's pleasure.

So why not let her serve her Mistress?

Simone locked eyes with Jade, her voice dropping to a whisper. "You want to serve me? Then you will serve me on your knees."

Jade exhaled softly. And without hesitation, she dropped to her knees.

Simone's pulse raced, satisfaction and desire surging through her veins. But she didn't let it show.

"Not there." Her eyes never leaving Jade's, she sauntered over to her desk and took her place behind it, a hand on the back of her chair. "Here."

Jade straightened up as if to rise to her feet, but a shake of Simone's head froze her in place.

"No," she said. "*Crawl.*"

A crimson flush rose up Jade's cheeks. Slowly, she got down on her hands and knees, lowered her head, and crawled across the marble floor, over the Persian rug underneath Simone's desk, stopping before her chair.

No, her *throne.*

Simone seated herself in it, gazing down at Jade kneeling before her, head bowed, eyes downcast, her dark hair flowing over her shoulders and back in a curtain of silk. *On her knees. At my feet. What a beautiful sight to behold.*

Simone leaned down, drawing her fingers up the center of Jade's throat and tilting her head up to look into her eyes.

"You are *divine,*" she said.

Jade's lips quivered, a soft breath escaping them. Simone released her chin and sat back in her chair, resting her arms on the armrests.

"Go on, princess," she said. "Serve me."

A fire flickered in Jade's eyes. Slowly, she took Simone's foot and removed her high-heeled shoe from it, setting it aside carefully before doing the same with the other shoe. Then she skimmed her hands up Simone's legs, up past her knees, up her thighs, pushing up her skirt.

Simone raised her hips from the chair, allowing Jade to slide her hands up to her waist. She hooked her fingers into the waistband of Simone's panties and pantyhose and drew them down her legs, pulling them from her feet and setting them next to her heels. Her panties were already wet.

"You see how wet you make me?" Simone said. "You see what you do to me?"

"Yes, Mistress," Jade murmured.

"Do you want to taste me?"

Jade nodded.

Simone leaned forward on her throne. "Beg for it."

Jade's breath hitched. Her head still bowed, she peered up at Simone with hooded eyes. "Please," she whispered. "I want you. I want to taste you. I want to serve you. I want to make you feel as good as you make me feel. *Please.*"

Simone shifted her hips forward, parting her legs before Jade's waiting lips.

"Go on," she said. "Taste me."

Jade exhaled slowly. Running her hands up the insides of Simone's legs, she leaned in close, breathing in her scent. Then she buried herself between Simone's thighs, tongue and lips stroking and circling and teasing her folds.

A moan erupted from Simone's chest. "That's it. Make me come like that night in the hotel. Make me scream so loud they'll hear us ten floors down."

Jade had always been one to rise to a challenge. Clutching firmly onto Simone's thighs, she dragged her tongue up to Simone's clit, flicking and swirling. Simone closed her eyes and leaned back in her chair, letting heavenly tremors ripple through her.

"God..." She tipped her head back, her hands gripping her armrests. "That feels exquisite."

She rocked her hips, pushing back against Jade's mouth. As her thighs began to tremble, she moved her hands to the top of Jade's head, her fingers curling through her hair, grasping handfuls of it as she pushed and pulled, guiding her, urging her on.

Faster. Slower. Yes, right there. She didn't need to say a word. Jade was her devoted servant. She could read Simone's body as well as Simone could read hers. They were so in sync, so utterly intertwined, that pleasuring each other was as natural as breathing.

"Yes," Simone panted, her thighs clenching around Jade's head. "Yes, yes!"

One more sweep of Jade's tongue was all it took to send Simone tumbling over the edge. A cry flew from her lips as pleasure overtook her, flooding her whole body. Her hips arched, her fingers tightening around Jade's hair in an unspoken command. *Don't stop. Don't stop until I've given you every last drop of pleasure. Don't stop until your queen is sated.*

After an eternity of bliss, she sank back into her chair, breathless and weak. But not too weak to pull Jade to her feet and draw her onto her lap.

"You have no idea what you do to me," Simone murmured. "No idea how much you make me lose myself."

Jade bit her lip. "After that, I think I have some idea."

Simone smothered her words with a greedy kiss. No, Jade had no idea what she was doing to Simone. Making her feel more alive than ever. Making her want something *more*. Making her question everything she believed.

Love is a lie. Love makes you weak. It will only end in betrayal.

Could she trust Jade not to burn her?

CHAPTER 24

Just do it. Just press send.

Jade stared at the email draft on her screen. It was mid-afternoon, and while the day was far from over, she'd managed to finish almost everything Simone had asked her to do. And since Simone was in a meeting with the legal department, Jade was taking the time to work on something else, something unrelated to her job.

She scanned the email again. She'd written it the morning after she spent the night at Simone's mansion. That night had given her the confidence to do what she'd been afraid to do for so long. It was time to take control. Of her life. Of her past.

It was time to report Philippa for what she'd done to her.

But Jade still had her doubts, still had questions niggling at the back of her mind. So the email had sat in her drafts, unsent, for more than a week. She'd read it over and over, but she hadn't been able to bring herself to send it.

She leaned back in her chair and stretched out her legs. What was holding her back? She wasn't afraid anymore. Or at the very least, her desire for Philippa to face some form of justice trumped her fears.

But justice wasn't the only thing Jade wanted. She wanted closure. Not an apology, or some sign of remorse. She would never get either from Philippa. No, what she wanted was catharsis. To free herself of everything to do with Philippa, every thought, every emotion she'd kept bottled up inside for the last two years.

She'd already gotten a hint of that when she told Simone about what had happened between them. But she needed something more. She needed to look Philippa in the eye and say everything she'd ever wanted to say to her. To give voice to all the anger and hurt Philippa had caused her. To tell her that she knew exactly what she was—a predator who preyed on naïve young women like Jade had once been.

To tell Philippa that she'd do everything in her power to make sure she got what she deserved.

First, I'll face her. Then I'll do what needs to be done.

Jade picked up her phone and opened up the private messaging app she and Philippa had used to communicate in secret. While she'd long deleted any trace of Philippa from her life, she'd been relieved to learn that deleting the app hadn't deleted all their old messages. She needed them to prove what had happened between them. And she could use the app to get Philippa's attention.

Jade typed out a message.

I've been thinking about you lately. I want to catch up. When can we meet?

She read over her message again. She needed to tread carefully. If it was obvious that the meeting wasn't going to be friendly, Philippa wouldn't agree to it.

Jade pressed send and let out a long, slow breath. This

was it. She was finally going to face *her*. That was, assuming Philippa wanted to see her at all. What if she ignored Jade's message entirely?

But barely five minutes later, a reply arrived.

I'm glad you reached out. I've missed you.

Was Philippa really acting like everything was okay between them? Knowing her the way Jade did, Philippa truly believed she'd done nothing wrong. How had Jade ever fallen for the woman's false words?

Another message popped up on her phone screen.

I'd love to see you again. Let's meet on Friday after work. 7 p.m. at The Fox?

The Fox was a bar downtown. And while it wouldn't have been Jade's meeting place of choice, it was public enough that if things went sideways, she'd be safe.

Sounds great. I'll see you then.

She pressed send. Not a moment later, Simone strode into the room.

"Christ, that was dull. If I wanted to hear about the minutiae of contract law, I'd have gone to law school." She shut the door behind her. "The good news is the Ashton Star acquisition is finalized. Settlement is on Friday. We'll meet with Ashton, sign on the dotted line, and she'll hand over the keys, so to speak. Then the hotel will be ours."

"That's great news!" Jade said. "It must feel amazing to finally have this deal done."

"You have no idea. And once everything with The Star is up and running, I can get the ball rolling on my East Coast expansion plans. Boston. Philadelphia. New York City. But I'm getting ahead of myself." Simone perched on the edge of Jade's desk, facing her. "This calls for celebration. After work on Friday, we'll go out for dinner, just the two of us, somewhere nice. And then?" She reached down, drawing her fingers up the base of Jade's chin. "We'll see where the night takes us."

Simone leaned in to kiss her. But before their lips could meet, Jade drew back reluctantly.

"That sounds perfect, really," she said. "But I can't. I have plans after work on Friday."

"Plans that are more important than celebrating our achievement?" Simone asked. "After all, you deserve it. You put plenty of work into this, too."

Jade gave her an apologetic shrug. "I'd reschedule, but it's important." She had the chance to confront Philippa, to put everything that had happened between them to rest. She couldn't let it pass her by. And she couldn't afford to wait, couldn't risk losing her resolve.

Simone frowned. "It's nothing serious, is it?"

Jade hesitated. A part of her wanted to tell Simone everything. But it had been hard enough to tell her about Philippa in the first place. And while Simone had been careful to hide her disdain for the woman, Jade had sensed it. Would Simone think her weak for going back to Philippa for closure?

Jade shook her head. "It's nothing. And it probably won't take too long. We could celebrate afterward. Or on the weekend?"

"It's fine," Simone said. "We'll see."

Silence fell over them. Simone stood up from the desk. And as she did, her eyes flicked to Jade's laptop screen. Her personal inbox was still open.

She closed the window. "Just checking some emails. Sorry, I know I shouldn't be doing that on the clock."

Simone folded her arms across her chest. "As long as you

get your work done, I don't care what else you do. Speaking of which, did you forward me that email about the Silver Lake site?"

"I'll send it to you now."

Simone gave her a nod and returned to her desk. But even from a distance, Jade could feel something radiating from her. Irritation? Anger?

Jade's heart sank. Was Simone angry at her for telling her *no* for what had to be the first time? Was she upset that Jade wasn't making herself available to serve her every whim?

No, Jade was being crazy. Sure, Simone was strict. A control freak, even. But she'd never been *controlling*.

Yet Jade couldn't help but think back to the way Philippa had gone silent and cold on her whenever she didn't do what Philippa wanted.

Jade shook her head. Everything that was happening with Philippa had brought all her insecurities to the surface. It was making her see things that weren't there.

Philippa had left her with a shattered heart. And if it was ever going to be whole again, if Jade was ever going to trust anyone again, she needed to face her.

CHAPTER 25

Ashton folded her hands on the mahogany conference room table. "Take all the time you need. I'm sure you'll find everything is in order."

Simone flipped through the pages of the contract. She was in the conference room of The Ashton Star, along with Jade, Ashton, and their respective legal teams. Through the windows behind them, the Los Angeles cityscape stretched out, bathed in the late morning sun.

Here Simone sat, in the heart of the city, on the top of the world, everything she'd ever worked for at the tip of her fingers.

All she had to do was sign on the dotted line.

She flipped to the last page and turned to Jade, who had a pen ready in her hand. Simone signed her name at the bottom of the page next to Ashton's, then shut the leather folder and slid it across the table. "It's done."

The contract was signed. The deal was settled.

The Star was hers.

Ashton took the folder and handed it to the man sitting beside her. "It was a pleasure doing business with you."

"The pleasure is all mine," Simone said.

She rose to her feet. Now that the hotel was hers, she didn't have a moment to waste. She needed to get the ball rolling on bringing her vision for The Star to life. There were applications to file, plans to approve. All the while, she needed to ensure the hotel continued running smoothly. She wanted to keep it open until the very moment renovations started.

As everyone filed toward the door, Ashton shook Simone's hand firmly. "I'm looking forward to seeing what you do with the hotel. After how hard you pushed me to sell it to you, I have high expectations."

"Let me assure you," Simone said, "The Star is in good hands."

Ashton gave her a small smile. "It will take me a while to get used to the new name. But you're right. This hotel doesn't belong to the Ashtons anymore. It never did. It belongs to all of Los Angeles. So take good care of it."

"I will, Ashton. I will."

She released Simone's hand. "Go on ahead. I'm going to stay here and say goodbye to this place, if you don't mind."

"Of course. We'll give you some space."

"I appreciate it. All the best to you and your... assistant. You're very lucky to have each other."

She gave Jade a nod that might as well have been a wink. Especially given the way it made Jade blush. They'd been careful to remain professional in front of Ashton. How had she figured it out?

"And Simone?" she said.

"Yes?"

"If that club of yours is ever looking for investors, let me know."

Simone nodded and left the conference room, Jade at her heels, heading for the ground floor. It wasn't until they were in the back seat of her car, on the way back to the office with the privacy screen up, that Simone allowed herself to celebrate.

"It's done," she said. "It's finally done. I'm so thrilled, I could just—"

She took Jade's face in her hands, drawing her into a hot, hard kiss. Jade let out a muffled gasp. But her surprise only lasted a moment before she pressed her body back against Simone's, deepening the kiss, murmurs rising from her chest. Her lips were soft and supple, and eager, oh so eager.

Satisfaction rippled through Simone's body. She had everything she wanted in her hands. The Star. And Jade.

Sweet, beautiful Jade. As strong as she is submissive, as vulnerable as she is bold. She was everything Simone desired. And with each day that passed, that desire only grew. Simone wanted so badly to give in to those feelings. She wanted so badly to make Jade more than her assistant, her submissive.

She wanted so badly to make Jade hers.

But she'd learned long ago that that was a path to pain. Relationships never lasted. People only hurt her.

Would Jade be any different?

Simone pushed the thought aside, breaking the kiss. "An occasion like this calls for a celebration. Why don't we have one of our own, right here, right now?"

A smile crossed Jade's lips. "What did you have in mind?"

Simone glanced out the window at the cars stalled around them. "In this traffic, I'd say we have ten minutes before we're back at the office." She turned back to Jade, leaning in close and sliding a hand up Jade's thigh. "That's more than enough time to make you come so hard you forget your own name."

Jade exhaled softly, her eyes shimmering with need. Simone ran her hands up to Jade's shoulders, pushing her backward, pinning her to the corner between the seat and the car door.

"The real question is," Simone said, "can you come without screaming so loud that everyone in the cars around us hears you?"

She didn't give Jade a chance to say a single word before drawing her hands down Jade's chest, skating them over her breasts and stomach, all the way to her thighs. She slipped her fingers underneath Jade's skirt, sliding them up to the waistband of her panties. Jade's breath hitched, her hips rising from the seat impatiently.

"Eager to get straight to business, I see," Simone said. "Luckily for you, so am I."

In one swift motion, she tore Jade's panties from her legs and pushed her knees apart, gliding her hand up the inside of her thigh, higher and higher until they reached the point where her legs met. Jade's chest heaved with deep breaths, her thighs trembling.

Simone slipped her hand between Jade's lower lips, her fingers grazing silken folds. Jade's head fell back as she parted her legs wider, spreading them out as far as she could.

"You're already wet. Is it the idea of someone hearing us that has you all worked up?" Simone teased her with long, slow strokes. "I quite like the idea. Of everyone on the street, in the cars around us, listening to me toy with my sweet princess. Of everyone hearing you come apart. Of everyone knowing you're *mine*."

She drew a finger up to Jade's clit, circling it gently. A moan rose from Jade's chest. She clamped her hand over her mouth, her eyes flicking toward the privacy screen.

"Oh?" Simone drew her hand back, tracing it down Jade's thigh, leaving a trail of wetness behind. "If you don't want anyone to hear you, I can stop."

Jade shook her head. "Don't stop," she panted. "Please don't stop."

Simone chuckled softly, slipping her fingers between Jade's legs once again, stroking and flicking, slowly at first, then faster. Jade lifted her hips, pushing back against Simone's hand. And when Simone slid her fingers inside her, her whole body shuddered, a whimper spilling from her lips.

"There's nothing sweeter than the sounds you make as you come undone," Simone purred. "And there's nothing more satisfying than feeling you unravel around my fingers."

She thrust her fingers deeper, delving and curling, the heel of her hand caressing Jade's clit. Jade shivered, her skin flushed with heat. Simone could feel how close she was to the edge, could feel Jade pulse and throb around her fingers, could feel the pressure building inside her.

"Oh…" Jade's hand slipped from her mouth. "Oh!"

Her body tensed, her hips rising from the seat as her pleasure peaked. Her back arched, her mouth falling open in a wordless cry of ecstasy. Simone moved inside her, feeling her tighten and release, tighten and release, over and over and over.

Until finally, Jade's body calmed, and she fell back into her seat, breathing hard and fast.

"Whew." Jade's hand fell to Simone's lap. "You should buy a hotel every day, because that was... wow."

"What did I tell you?" Simone murmured. "I said I'd make you come, and with three minutes to spare."

Jade opened her eyes, looking out the window. Traffic was moving again, and they were almost back at the office. She smoothed down her skirt, glancing frantically around the car.

"Looking for these?" Simone asked, dangling Jade's panties from her finger.

A pink flush rose up Jade's cheeks. She took her panties from Simone and slipped them back on. Simone leaned over and straightened up Jade's blouse before tucking a stray strand of her hair behind her ear.

"It's a pity you have plans this evening," Simone said. "Otherwise we could continue celebrating. In the penthouse of The Star, perhaps. A perk of owning the hotel means it's at my disposal whenever I want it, for whatever I want. Or *whoever* I want."

But the coy smile Simone was expecting didn't materialize. Instead, Jade glanced away, her fingers fidgeting in her lap.

"I'm sorry," she said. "I'd change my plans if I could."

"Jade, you don't need to apologize. I'm only teasing you."

"I can call you after I'm done. Maybe we can do something then?"

"Only if that's what you want. I don't want to get in the way of these plans of yours."

The car stopped in front of the office building. Jade didn't wait for the driver to open the door before getting out. Simone frowned. Bringing up the evening's plans had sucked all the air out of the car, along with the mood. And now, Jade could barely look at her.

What was going on? What were these plans that Jade was being so tight-lipped about? While they weren't any of Simone's business, it was unlike Jade to be so secretive.

What was she hiding?

CHAPTER 26

The afternoon came and went. And at 6:30 p.m., Jade announced that she was leaving.

Simone looked up from the file in front of her. "Are you forgetting something?"

"I don't think so." Jade's eyes narrowed in thought. "I sent those emails like you asked. I made dinner reservations at the French restaurant you like for next month when the investors from New York are in town. And I called the city about speeding up the development application for the Silver Lake site."

"The new floor plans for The Star. I asked you to print out a hard copy for me."

Jade grimaced. "I completely forgot. I sent it to the printer but got sidetracked. I'll grab it now."

Simone watched her slip out of the room. She'd been behaving strangely all afternoon. Jumpy. Distracted. Nervous. She was trying her best to hide it, but Simone could tell.

It had to have something to do with her plans for the

evening. Plans she clearly didn't want to tell Simone about. Not that she owed Simone an explanation. It wasn't like Jade was her girlfriend. They'd been clear about that from the start.

Simone refocused her attention on the document before her, minutes from a recent meeting. But as she made a note at the bottom of the page, the ink in her pen ran dry.

She tossed it into the trash can nearby and made her way to Jade's desk. Her ever-organized assistant had a virtual stationary closet in her bottom drawer.

Simone opened it up and grabbed a box of pens. As she closed the drawer again, her eyes landed on Jade's laptop. The screen was still on, a calendar displayed in the browser. But it wasn't Simone's calendar, which her assistant was in charge of managing. It was Jade's personal calendar.

And underneath today's date, the evening was blocked out for an event. There was no description, just a location.

7 p.m. The Fox.

Simone knew the place. Every gay and bisexual woman in Los Angeles did. And while the small venue wasn't officially a gay bar, it was a popular spot for women to meet and catch up. Or to hook up.

And that was where Jade was going.

Footsteps approached Simone's office. She straightened up just as Jade stepped through the door.

Simone held up the box of pens. "I took these from your desk. Get some more next time you're in the supply room." She returned to her desk, taking a seat behind it. "And bring that to me."

Jade set the rolled-up floor plans on Simone's desk. "Is there anything else you need?"

Simone shook her head. "Go. Enjoy your evening."

Jade returned to her desk and shut her laptop, packing it into her bag along with the rest of her things. She was almost out the door when she turned around and hurried back to Simone's desk, planting a rushed kiss on her cheek as she mumbled a goodbye.

Simone watched her leave. There was an anxiousness in her movements, her voice. An evasiveness, even.

It was the kind of evasiveness Simone was uncomfortably familiar with. She'd been hyper-attuned to it ever since she was a little girl dealing with her parents' fraught relationship, her father's cheating ways. She'd spotted it in negotiations and business deals, seeing through her competitors' lies. She could tell when someone was hiding something.

And Jade? She was hiding something.

Simone crossed her arms. Jade had no obligation to share what was going on in her personal life. But over the past months, they'd grown closer. They'd shared their darkest desires, their dreams. There was a bond between them, unspoken but strong.

And Simone longed to speak the words that would make that bond real. But that went against everything she'd ever learned, everything she'd experienced. Her parents' endless fights, their shouts echoing through the house as she cowered under her covers. Her father's secrets and lies, the way he'd make her keep his affairs secret from her mother, until finally, the truth came out, breaking their family apart.

Her mother, telling her that she could never, *ever* trust anyone. That love was a lie, that relationships only ever ended in heartbreak and betrayal.

Why would things with Jade be any different? Why

should Simone trust her? Jade had never given her a reason not to.

At least, until now.

7 p.m. The Fox. It was already quarter to 7, and the bar was a 15-minute drive away.

Simone stood up. She knew what she needed to do.

Simone arrived at the bar with a few minutes to spare, slipping through the doors at the heels of a group of women. While it was still early in the night, the small bar was already packed.

She edged around the crowd, finding a corner where she could see the entire room. It only took her a few seconds to find Jade. She sat alone at the bar, a drink before her, barely touched. She didn't look around, didn't glance at the door as if waiting for someone. She simply stared down into her glass.

Simone waited. And the longer she waited, the louder the voices warring in her mind became.

Coming here was a mistake.

I need to know what she's doing here.

Spying on her like this is wrong.

I need to know if I can trust her.

But all Simone's thoughts fell silent when she spotted a woman approaching Jade at the bar.

Simone studied her through narrowed eyes. She was on the shorter side, with reddish brown hair and pale skin. A stranger? A friend?

Something else?

Simone waited. Jade had her back to the woman, so she

didn't notice her. Not until the woman was standing right next to her.

Jade turned and spoke a single word. A greeting? The woman's name? Simone was too far away to hear, but she could see them clearly.

She watched as Jade gazed into the woman's eyes, hypnotized.

She watched as the woman stepped in close, her hand falling to Jade's waist as she spoke into her ear.

She watched as the woman reached for Jade's face and leaned in to kiss her...

Simone turned away, numbness spreading through her body. She'd seen all she needed to see.

Without looking back, she left the bar.

CHAPTER 27

The moment Philippa touched Jade, time froze.

It was just like that night at Club Velvet when the dark-haired woman approached her. Just like the first time Philippa kissed her when they were alone in her office one night. Just like every time in Jade's life when she'd been too afraid to make waves.

But this time? She pushed back.

Physically, shoving Philippa away before their lips could touch.

"Stop!" Jade stepped back and crossed her arms. "Just stop!"

"Okay, okay." Philippa held up her hands. "I'm just happy to see you again, that's all. I've missed you, Jade."

Anger roiled in Jade's stomach. Did Philippa think they would simply pick up where they'd left off? Did she think that after everything she'd done, Jade would go weak-kneed at the sight of her like she was still that naïve student with a crush?

She took a deep breath. If she wanted the chance to

speak her mind, she needed to keep her cool. And she wouldn't give Philippa the satisfaction of getting under her skin.

"I just want to talk," Jade said. "Let's go somewhere quieter."

Philippa nodded. "Let me get a drink first."

A few agonizing minutes later, they were seated at a table in the courtyard at the back of the bar.

"Here we are again," Philippa said. "It's been so long since we last spoke. Miss me, did you? Or is there some other reason you wanted to see me?"

Jade took a swig of her drink, fortifying herself. "I have some things to say to you. Things I need to get off my chest."

Philippa rolled her eyes. "Is this about the research project? You're not still upset about that, are you?"

"This isn't about the research project. Well, it isn't only about that. It's about how you *used* me the entire time we were together."

For a moment, Philippa looked hurt. "I used you? Jade, how can you say that? How can you even think that? I *loved* you. Didn't you love me, too?"

Jade shook her head. "It doesn't matter what either of us felt. You were my professor. My adviser. You were supposed to be looking out for me. Instead, you took advantage of how naïve and impressionable I was, coercing me into this messed-up relationship with you. And that was wrong."

"Oh please. You didn't have any objections at the time."

"How could I? How could I when you never allowed me to have any feelings or opinions of my own? When you would force me to do whatever you wanted?"

"I never forced you to do anything. And I certainly never

ANNA STONE

forced you to be with me. You wanted me. Your little crush was obvious from day one. You practically threw yourself at me." Philippa picked up her drink, swirling it around before taking a sip. "And if you were so unhappy, you could have ended things. But you didn't. You were with me because you wanted to be."

"All this time, I thought the same thing. But it's taken me two years to realize that the entire time we were together, I was trapped. No, you never forced me to be with you. But you manipulated me into feeling like I couldn't say no, which is the same thing. I never had a choice, not really. And you made that clear when you threatened to ruin my life if I ever told anyone about us."

"Jade, when I said those things, I didn't mean them. I was scared. Scared of what would happen if anyone found out about us. I'd never do anything to hurt you—"

"All you ever did was hurt me, Philippa. All the while convincing me that the way you treated me was okay. You never cared about my feelings. You never cared about what I wanted. It was about what *you* wanted from *me*. You were a bully, grinding down everything I was until there was nothing left of me at all."

Philippa opened her mouth to speak, but Jade didn't let her.

"And you knew it. It's why you went after me in the first place. You knew that I was so infatuated with you that I'd do whatever you told me to because I was so desperate to please you. That I'd never stand up for myself because I was scared of upsetting you." Jade's hands curled into fists on the table. "But I'm done. I'm done trying to please everyone. I'm done being too afraid to make waves. I'm done being ashamed of what you did to me. You're a predator, Philippa. And I'm going to make sure everyone knows it."

Philippa tensed. "What are you talking about?"

"What do you think? I'm doing what I should have done years ago. I'm reporting you."

"You wouldn't *dare*." Philippa's eyes narrowed to slits. "Who's going to believe a word you say? Especially without any proof?"

"You don't think all those messages we sent each other are proof enough?"

Philippa scoffed. "You think our messages are going to do you any favors? All they'll do is show everyone how obsessed you were with me."

"You can try to twist it all you want. But the truth is a powerful thing. And once it's out there, there's no putting it back in the box. Everyone will know what you've done. And whether they believe it or not, it will be a blemish on your name that will make people think twice about you. Especially any students you try to pull the same thing on. Because I'm willing to bet I wasn't the first, or the last."

Philippa didn't deny it. "So what, you're going to try to ruin my reputation? The only person who'll be ruined by this is you, the dirty little whore who seduced me."

Jade crossed her arms. "You tried that line on me two years ago. It's not going to work again. But we'll find out if what you say is true soon enough."

Philippa frowned. "What does that mean?"

"Oh, did I say I'm *going to* report you? I should have said that I *already* reported you. I sent the email before I came here."

Jade had left it as late as possible so she wouldn't tip Philippa off. It had been the most nerve-racking thing she'd ever done. She'd spent the afternoon so overwhelmed with anxiety that she'd almost called everything off.

But she'd done it. She'd sent the email to her grad school's Title IX office. She'd come to The Fox.

And now, facing Philippa, she was fearless.

The color drained from the woman's face. "What have you done?"

"What I should have done years ago." Jade stood up, her fingers splayed on the table before her. "Everyone is going to know the truth. Everyone is going to know what you've done. And even if it's too late for me, I'll do everything in my power to stop you from doing the same thing to anyone else. You're not going to get away with it again."

"You bitch." Philippa's face turned red. "You lying bitch! You'll regret this. I'll make sure of it! No one is going to believe you! No one—"

But Jade didn't hear the rest of Philippa's words. Because she was already walking away.

It wasn't until she was out on the sidewalk at the front of the bar that she allowed herself to breathe again. She'd done it. She'd confronted Philippa, vanquished her, banished her to the past where she belonged. She'd let go of all her anger, and shame, and hurt. She'd conquered the one thing that was holding her back.

And there was only one person she wanted to share this moment with. One person she wanted to share this victory with. One woman who had captivated her mind, her body, her everything, from the moment they met. A woman so in tune with Jade's every desire that she'd uncovered depths of not only vulnerability, but strength, that Jade hadn't known she possessed.

A woman who had been there for her, without fail, whenever Jade needed her.

Her hands shaking with adrenaline, she took out her phone and called Simone. With luck, she'd still be at the office and they could meet up downtown.

But the phone rang and rang, until finally, the call went to voicemail.

She frowned. Simone always answered Jade's calls, no matter the time of day. And Simone's schedule was clear all evening.

Maybe something came up. Jade left her a message, then hung up the phone and slipped it back into her purse. She'd have to wait a little longer to see Simone.

But when she did, she would tell her everything. That she'd faced Philippa. That Simone had given her the confidence to do it. That she wanted to move on, move forward, not only with her life, but in her relationship with Simone.

And Jade would finally tell her how she felt about her.

CHAPTER 28

F riday night passed. So did Saturday. So did most of Sunday.

And Jade didn't hear a single word from Simone.

"I tried calling her, sending her messages, and nothing," she told Renee, who was at the other end of the video call. "She always gets back to me quickly, so when she didn't, I started freaking out. I thought something had happened to her."

After all, that was the most obvious explanation. Why else would Simone stop responding to her so suddenly?

"Then I figured I was probably overreacting, so I decided to wait. But it's been two days now. She's blowing me off. And I have no idea why." Jade folded her legs underneath her on her bed. "Everything seemed fine when I last saw her. Except she did seem kind of upset that I couldn't spend Friday night with her because I had plans. That can't be why, though. Who would be so petty? So manipulative?"

Philippa, that's who. She'd always gotten upset when Jade didn't do what she wanted. She'd tell Jade she wasn't mad, all the while acting cold and withholding. And in the end, Jade would always give in and apologize, even if she'd done nothing wrong.

Until one day, she'd refused. And that was when Philippa kicked her to the curb. Because what use was Jade to her if she didn't bow to her wishes?

But Simone wasn't like Philippa. She wasn't using Jade for her own pleasure. She would never toss Jade aside because she wouldn't serve her every whim.

But what other explanation did she have?

"If she thinks she can treat me like this," Jade said. "If she thinks she can just use me and throw me away like a piece of trash—"

"Whoa, hold on," Renee interrupted. "Don't you think you're being a little hasty? Whatever is going on, I'm sure there's an explanation."

"If there is, why isn't Simone telling me what it is? Why is she leaving me in the dark like this? Why am I sitting here wondering if she's going to call me like some love-struck idiot?"

"You're right, it's not cool what she's doing. But you're going to see her at work tomorrow, right? You should talk to her then."

But Jade wasn't going to wait. She wasn't going to stand for this. She wasn't going to let Simone treat her this way, let anyone treat her this way, ever again. And she wasn't going to fall apart.

No, this time, she was going to take matters into her own hands.

"If Simone won't speak to me, I want to know why," she said. "And I'm going to find out."

"Uh, how do you plan to do that?" Renee asked.

"I'm going to go to her. I have her schedule. I know exactly where she'll be tonight. I'm going to show up, and I'm going to get her attention one way or another."

"Wait, where is she going to be tonight? Where are you going?"

Jade got up from her bed. "I'm going to Club Velvet."

An hour later, Jade strode through the doors of Club Velvet, Renee at her heels.

"You didn't have to come with me," Jade muttered.

"Yes, I did," Renee said. "Someone has to make sure you don't do anything stupid."

"I'm not going to do anything stupid, Ree."

For some reason, her friend seemed to think that she wasn't in her right mind. But if anything, Jade's mind was clearer than ever. Meeting with Philippa hadn't only given her closure. It had reminded her that she needed to keep her guard up.

It had reminded her that she could never let anyone do what Philippa had done to her ever again.

She marched to the bar and ordered a drink. It was a Sunday evening, so the club wasn't busy, but there were still plenty of people around. And they all seemed to be couples, kissing, touching, playing. A few who were daring enough were doing far more. This was nothing like the opening night party, where no sex was allowed. Tonight, in this den of debauchery, nothing was off limits.

And in coming here, Jade was sending a message of defiance to the woman who was supposed to be her Mistress.

I'm here without you. I'm free for the taking. Don't like it? Come and claim me.

Yes, Jade was provoking her. Yes, she was trying to get Simone's attention in her little black dress and heels, exuding the kind of sensual confidence she'd never possessed until she met Simone. Yes, she was playing games. But only because Simone was playing games with her, too.

She swallowed her drink in one long gulp, then gestured to the bartender, ordering another.

"Whoa," Renee said. "Slow down. You're acting crazy. This isn't you."

"No, this *is* me," Jade said. "This is who I am. And what would you know? You act like I'm still the girl I was in freshman year. You don't know me. You don't know what I've gone through. You don't know who I am anymore!"

Renee threw her hands up. "Because you don't talk to me! You don't tell me anything, not anymore. How the hell am I supposed to know what's going on with you when you're so closed off all the time? I don't know what happened to you, but you changed, Jade. We used to be best friends, but you shut me out. It's like you're a complete stranger! And this, the way you're acting, I'm not sure I like the person you are right now."

Jade winced. "I didn't know you felt that way."

Renee's face fell. "I'm sorry. I shouldn't have said all that."

"It's fine. You were just being honest."

"I didn't mean it. I was—"

"I said, *it's fine.* Look, I really can't do this right now. I just need some space, okay?"

"Sure. But I drove you here. Why don't I give you a ride home?"

Jade shook her head. "I just want to be alone."

"If that's what you want. I'm going to stick around and mingle for a while. I'll be here if you need me." She put a hand on Jade's arm. "And again, I'm sorry."

Jade turned back to the bar. And with a murmured goodbye, Renee disappeared into the crowd.

Jade sipped her drink, trying to wash away the sting of Renee's words. But her friend was right. These last few years, Jade had been so wrapped up in her problems that she'd let them consume her. She'd been so self-centered and closed off that she'd pushed Renee away, along with everyone else.

But she was trying to change. She was trying to let people in again. Hadn't she done that with Simone? Opened up to her, opened her heart to her?

And this is what I get?

Jade took another gulp of her drink and looked around the club. She couldn't see Simone anywhere. But she had to be here. She had the evening blocked off for an informal meeting with the other owners of Club Velvet.

Did she know that Jade was here?

Did she even care?

As Jade took another sip of her drink, she looked up at the glass-walled room at the far end of the club, high above the main floor. There were a handful of women gathered in it. And among them, leaning against the glass, a drink in her hand, was a statuesque woman in a dark dress, her blonde hair pulled back into a bun. Jade couldn't see her face, but she'd recognize her anywhere.

Simone.

Jade chugged the rest of her drink, then turned to the bartender and ordered another.

You want me, Mistress? Come and get me.

CHAPTER 29

Simone watched the crowd down in the club below, a glass of champagne in her hand. Elle had ordered a bottle to celebrate Simone's acquisition of The Ashton Star.

But Simone had steered the conversation toward club business as quickly as possible. She wasn't in the mood to celebrate.

"Simone? Are you listening?"

She turned away from the glass, focusing her attention on the other owners of Club Velvet, who sat gathered around a table. It was Olivia who had spoken to her. In her designer pantsuit and heels, her dark hair flowing down one shoulder, olive-brown skin glowing in the dim lighting of the club, she gave off the distinct impression that she'd just stepped off a private jet. Knowing Olivia, she likely had.

"I'm listening," Simone said. "What is it?"

"The situation with the bar staff?" When she didn't respond, Olivia continued. "We've lost three since we opened. Apparently, they didn't have the constitution for working at a place like this."

"We'll hire replacements. And up the base pay rate for new hires *and* the existing staff. If we want the best, the pay needs to reflect that."

Olivia nodded. "That should help. Our pay rate is already higher than most upscale establishments, so we'll have no shortage of applicants."

"I'll spread the word that we're hiring," Elle said. "There are always staff at my other clubs who are looking for extra work. And this time, so we don't run into this problem again, we should make sure any potential hires know exactly what they're getting into working at Club Velvet."

"And how do you propose we do that?" Valerie asked.

"By giving them a taste of what goes on here, of course. I'd be happy to give any new hires a hands-on demonstration."

"Yes, because that's what we need," Valerie murmured. "You domming our new employees."

"I wasn't suggesting that, exactly." Elle crossed one leg over the other. "But it would be effective, wouldn't it? If they can't handle the heat, they're not cut out to work here."

"And this is why HR has a collective stroke whenever anyone mentions your name," Valerie said.

Olivia held up her hands. "Can we stay on topic? It was hard enough getting everyone here tonight. We haven't had the chance to sit down together and talk club business since opening night."

Opening night. The night that had changed everything. The night Simone had met Jade.

But she couldn't think about that right now. Because that would mean facing up to everything that had happened over the last two days.

However, Simone would need to confront reality sooner

rather than later. Because tomorrow morning, she would see Jade face to face. And she wouldn't be able to ignore the truth any longer.

"Now, is there anything else we need to discuss?" Olivia asked. "Simone, you haven't said much tonight."

"There's nothing to say," Simone replied. "Everything is running smoothly."

"Then why don't we call it a night? I'm just dying to get home and have a long, hot shower."

Elle rose to her feet. "If we're done here, I caught the eye of a cute butch on my way in. She seemed *very* interested in the impact play setup. I'm going to go see if she needs some help." She raised her champagne flute in Simone's direction. "Congratulations again on the acquisition."

The others followed suit, raising their glasses and finishing off their champagne. Olivia and Elle said their goodbyes and headed down the stairs, leaving Simone and Valerie alone.

"You don't have to run off too?" Simone asked.

"Not tonight. The new nanny is on." Valerie joined her by the glass, draping her arms over the railing as she surveyed the club below. "Tonight belongs to Madame V."

"And how is the new nanny going?" Valerie had high standards when it came to her daughter.

"Hazel seems to like her."

"And you?"

"She's good. *Very* good." Valerie straightened up, turning to Simone. "But that's enough about me. What about you? You have that look about you, like there's something on your mind."

Simone didn't miss the abrupt change of subject. "I'm simply swamped with work right now, that's all."

"Simone, you just closed on the biggest deal of your career. You bought *The Ashton Star*. You should be celebrating. Instead, you're acting like your pet died. Maybe the others didn't notice, but I did."

Simone sipped her champagne. She'd barely drunk any of it. "Like I said, I have a lot going on right now."

"Like what? Come on, Simone. I know you're not one for talking about your problems, but we've known each other for years. You're one of my closest friends. You can talk to me."

Simone let out a heavy sigh. "It's about Jade."

"You mean your assistant? Who is also your sub? Who you've also been sleeping with?"

"No need to remind me what a bad idea that was," Simone said.

Valerie held up her hands apologetically. "Go on."

"Well, I saw her on Friday night at The Fox. She was with another woman, and they kissed." Simone shook her head. "It doesn't make sense. It doesn't make sense that she would do that."

Jade, her loyal, devoted princess. She'd never given Simone any reason not to trust her. She'd never kept secrets from her.

She'd never turn to another woman, not when she'd promised herself to Simone.

But Simone had seen it plain as day. And ever since, she'd been numb with denial. It didn't seem real. It couldn't have been real.

Or was she only telling herself that because she couldn't stomach the truth?

"Have you talked to her about it?" Valerie asked.

"I haven't been able to bring myself to. Because even if

there's an explanation for it, it doesn't change the way it's made me feel. Uncertain, unsure, off-balance. And I don't like feeling this way. I don't like how crazy she makes me. I don't like that I want to be with her so badly that it *consumes* me." Simone gripped the railing in front of her, her voice rising. "And I don't like that all of this is out of my control, that in an instant, it can all come undone. Because everything I feel for her, everything I feel when she's by my side, makes everything else in the world seem meaningless."

Silence fell over them, the music from the club below thumping in time with Simone's racing pulse. She released her grip on the railing, her knuckles white.

"Simone." Valerie put a hand on her arm. "You're in love."

Simone shook her head. "I care about her, I do. But *love*?"

"Do you really not see it? It's so obvious that you're in love with her. And I get it. I understand how terrifying that is. The last woman I loved? You know how that worked out. So I understand that it's easier to ignore those feelings. I understand that it's easier to shut them out, shut *her* out, rather than face her."

Simone grimaced. Hearing it out loud made it hard to deny her cowardice.

"But if you care about her at all?" Valerie said. "If you have any feelings for her? You need to talk to her before it's too late."

"You've certainly changed your tune." Simone crossed her arms. "Last time we talked about this, you warned me not to get involved with her. That it was too risky."

Valerie turned to look at the club beneath them. "Let's just say I'm starting to realize that sometimes, it's worth the risk."

"Perhaps." Simone cast her eyes over the crowd below once again. "Or perhaps—"

But before she could finish her thought, her eyes fell upon a woman sitting at the bar. Long dark hair, hanging loose down her back. A little black dress that caressed her every curve. And as she flicked her hair behind her shoulder, Simone caught a glimpse of her face.

Jade.

And she wasn't alone. Another woman stood beside her, leaning casually against the bar. Even from a distance, the woman's body language was clear.

She was hitting on Jade.

Simone tensed. It was just like the night they met. Just like the moment she first laid eyes on Jade from this very spot. And just like that night, it stirred every protective, possessive instinct in her.

Jade was *hers*. Simone needed to find out why she did what she did.

She needed to face her.

She turned to Valerie. "You know what? You're right." She downed the rest of her champagne. "I'm going to talk to Jade."

CHAPTER 30

"Just one drink," the woman said, running her hand through her short blonde hair. "I'm sure I can make you change your mind."

Jade stared pointedly ahead. "No, thanks. I'm not interested."

"Come on, live a little. Isn't that what you're here for? Why else would you come to a place like this all alone?"

Irritation rose inside her. This woman wasn't taking a hint.

And Jade was done being polite.

She downed the rest of her drink, slammed her glass down on the bar, and turned to the woman, shooting her a steely glare. "I told you, I'm *not interested*. So leave me the hell alone!"

"Jeez," the woman said. "No need to yell,"

"Obviously I do need to yell, because you're still standing here." Jade crossed her arms. "Go. Away."

"Okay, okay." Muttering under her breath, the woman grabbed her drink from the bar and walked away.

As Jade watched her disappear into the crowd, she spotted another blonde-haired woman standing just a few feet away.

Simone. And she was looking right at Jade.

Simone joined her at the bar. "Was she bothering you?"

Jade gestured to the bartender, who began pouring her another drink. "Why do you care?"

"I care because you're *mine*. And I care about you."

"You have some way of showing it."

The bartender handed Jade her drink and disappeared to the other end of the bar, no doubt sensing the tension in the air.

"Listen," Simone said. "We need to talk."

Jade scoffed. "Oh, so now you want to talk to me? After you ignored my calls and messages all weekend? Why should I listen to you? Why shouldn't I just tell you where to go?"

"If you'll give me a chance to explain—"

"It's been two days, Simone. Two days! Can you believe I was actually worried about you, at first? I thought something awful had happened to you. But then I realized you were just ignoring me. Then I realized you'd shut me out on purpose." Jade swirled her drink around and took a sip. "Well, I got your message loud and clear."

Simone glanced at Jade's glass. "How much have you had to drink tonight?"

"I'm *not* drunk. If anything, my head is clearer than ever. I came here to find you, but now that you're here? Now that I'm looking at you? I've realized I don't want to talk to you at all. I don't want to hear your excuses. I don't want anything to do with you. So leave me alone!"

Silence stretched out. As the seconds passed, Jade

assumed that Simone had done exactly what she'd told her to do.

Then, Simone spoke.

"Look at me."

Jade's stomach flipped. She kept her eyes pointed toward the bar, resisting the command in Simone's voice.

"I said, *look at me*, Jade."

She gripped her glass tightly. But she couldn't fight herself. Even now, she couldn't disobey her Mistress.

Jade turned to face her. "What do you—"

"I am *not* playing games," Simone said sharply. "I am trying to *fix* this. And you wouldn't be here if you didn't want that too. So stop being a brat and listen to me."

"*Fine.* I'm listening. Say whatever you want to say."

"Not here. Come with me. Leave your drink."

Jade took another swig of her drink before putting it down and following her. She hated the way she responded to Simone's commands instinctively, hated the way her body still burned for her.

Jade was still under her spell. And Simone was right. No small part of her still hoped—prayed—that Simone really could fix things like she always did.

But what could she possibly have to say that could make everything okay between them?

A minute later, they stepped into one of the club's private rooms. Just like the room Simone had taken her into that night so long ago, it was equipped with all kinds of kinky toys and tools. But unlike that night, they didn't excite her. Instead, they reminded her of all the ways she'd given herself to Simone, only to have Simone treat her like she was nothing.

Simone gestured toward the bed. "Sit."

Jade did as she was told, crossing her arms and glaring back at Simone, who stood looming over her.

"You wanted to talk," Jade said. "So talk."

Simone crossed her arms. "I'm sorry. I'm sorry I haven't been answering your calls. I'm sorry I ignored your messages. But I needed some space after…"

"After what?" Jade had never seen Simone lost for words before. It was unsettling.

"After I saw you on Friday night. With another woman."

"Another woman? What are you talking about?"

"At The Fox. I saw you kiss her."

"Wait." Jade blinked. "Are you talking about *Philippa*?"

Simone's face clouded over. "That was Philippa?"

"Yes, it was. And I don't know what you think you saw, but I didn't kiss her. *She* tried to kiss *me*, but I pushed her away, and then I gave her a piece of my mind. That's why I met with her in the first place! So I could finally tell her that what she did to me was wrong. So I could tell her I'd reported her to the school and everyone would know what she did. And you'd know this if you'd just answered your phone on Friday night when I tried to call you and tell you about it!"

She took a deep breath, trying to keep her calm. But all the emotions that had been building inside her for days were threatening to boil over.

Simone shook her head, speaking softly. "I've been such a fool. I knew you would never do that to me. I knew I should have trusted you. But when I saw you with her—"

"With Philippa?" Jade said. "With the woman who shattered my heart so badly that I spent years picking up the pieces of my life?"

"I didn't know who she was. I thought she was just another woman."

"And you thought I was seeing her behind your back? After I promised to be yours and yours alone? How could you even think that? How could you think I would do that to you?"

"It was a mistake! I know that now. But you'd been behaving so strangely for days, acting nervous, keeping things from me. And when I saw your calendar on your laptop, saw where you were going on Friday evening, I thought the worst. I needed to know if I could trust you, so I followed you. It was wrong, and I know it."

Jade spoke through gritted teeth. "Let me get this straight. You saw that I was anxious and there was something I wasn't telling you, so you decided I was hiding things from you. You took my laptop and went through my personal calendar. You followed me in secret and saw me with another woman, one who tried to kiss me *against my will*, so you thought I was cheating on you. And instead of talking to me about it, you ghosted me?"

"Yes, but—"

"How could you do that to me, knowing how Philippa treated me? Knowing that she took advantage of her power over me, using me for sex and then throwing me away?"

Horror dawned on Simone's face. "Jade, I am so, so sorry. I never considered how it would make you feel. I was so caught in my head. I saw my worst fears playing out before my eyes, and I couldn't think clearly."

Jade hesitated. "What do you mean?"

"I've told you about my parents. About their divorce, about how messy it was. It was because of my father's infidelity. Long before the divorce, I spent years being dragged around by my father while he sneaked around with his mistresses. He made me his accomplice, bribing me not to tell my mother, even threatening me.

"But eventually, she found out. And after she left him, she became bitter and hateful, constantly telling me that all our problems were caused by my cheating scumbag of a father. That I couldn't trust him, or anyone else. That love was a lie, and that everyone would betray me in the end. Her words poisoned me. And the girlfriends I had in my younger days proved those words to be true. So I gave up on relationships. I gave up on love. I gave up on ever opening my heart up to anyone." She looked deep into Jade's eyes. "But then, I met you."

Jade's heart skipped. Why did Simone's gaze still have the power to make her weak?

"These past months we've spent together have made me feel things I never thought I'd feel, want things I never thought I'd want," Simone said. "Because I want more than what we have, Jade. So much more."

Jade's stomach fluttered. Hadn't she thought the same thing just days ago? Hadn't she desperately wanted to tell Simone how she felt?

"But I began to doubt those feelings. I began to doubt myself. And when you started behaving the way you did, I began to doubt you. Then I saw you with her, and I pushed you away because I couldn't bear to have my heart ripped out. I let my insecurities get the best of me, and I'm sorry."

Silence fell over them, hanging heavy like a fog. But Jade could hear the rush of blood in her ears, the anger coursing through her body.

"You think I don't understand what that's like?" she whispered. "You think I don't know how it feels to be utterly terrified of falling for someone because they're only going to tear my heart out again?" Her hands curled around the bedsheets beneath her, gripping them tightly. "Of course I know what that feels like! I've felt that way for the past two years! But you know what I did? I chose to deal with it, face it head-on, instead of letting it control me. But you? You chose to betray my trust instead. And that's not okay. No matter what you've been through, it doesn't give you the right to treat me the way you did."

"I know, Jade. If I could take it all back, I would."

"But you can't," Jade said. "You can't."

"Then tell me what I need to do to make this right."

Jade shook her head. "It's already too late." Something squeezed inside her chest. "I trusted you. I gave myself to you. Despite everything I've been through, I made myself vulnerable to you in ways most people could never even imagine. I wanted so badly to be *yours*. And now this…"

"Jade—"

"I can't do this. Not anymore. I'm not going to leave you without an assistant. I'll do the job I was hired to do. I'll stay until your assistant gets back. I'll finish out the week. But that's all. That's all you're going to get from me. As far as you and I are concerned? We're done."

"Jade, please," Simone said softly.

"I'm sorry, but this is what I want. And I won't let anyone stomp all over me ever again." Jade stood up from the bed. "Good night, Simone. I'll see you tomorrow morning."

Without giving her a chance to say a single word, Jade marched to the door and left the room, leaving Simone, and any feelings she still had for her, behind.

CHAPTER 31

*J*ust one more day.

That was what Jade told herself every morning as she got ready for work. *Just one more day. Then another. Then another. Then the week will be over. Everything will be over.*

She could have quit her job that night at Club Velvet so she'd never have to see Simone's face again. After all, that was what she did after things ended with Philippa.

But not this time. This time, she refused to run away. This time, she refused to give in to shame. She would do her job. She would stay until the very end.

So every day, she dragged herself to work, put her head down, and powered through. She completed every task Simone gave her to her impossible standard, without complaint. She buried her feelings deep inside, numbing herself to everything. Because it was the only way she could face another day, face Simone, without breaking down.

Until at last, Friday arrived. And at 5 p.m. sharp, Simone summoned Jade to her desk.

Jade obeyed, one last time.

"Here." Simone slid an envelope across the desk toward her. "A letter of recommendation, from me, personally. To help you with any future job applications."

Jade picked up the envelope. "Thank you."

"It's the least I can do. I haven't told you enough how valuable you've been to me these past months. I know that working for me isn't easy, but you've always gone above and beyond. I dare say you've done an even better job than my regular assistant. So if there's anything I can do to help you find a new position, let me know. I have connections in the industry, so I can give you some leads, put in a good word for you."

Jade shook her head. "I'd rather find something myself."

"I'm sure you will, soon enough. And Jade?"

"Yes?"

"Thank you," Simone said. "For staying this week."

Jade glanced to the side. "I was just doing my job. Besides, you needed the help. I wasn't going to leave you in the lurch. You wouldn't have found anyone to replace me for just a week."

"Whatever your reasons, I'm grateful. And know this, Jade." Simone looked up at her, her eyes piercing straight into Jade's heart. "No one could ever replace you. No one."

Jade's breath caught in her chest. And for a moment, all the words that had gone unspoken hung in the air between them.

For a moment, all she wanted was for Simone to finally say those words out loud.

Instead, her boss gave her a polite nod. "Goodbye, Jade. I wish you the best."

Jade gathered her things from her desk, packing them

into a box. And without looking back, she left Simone's office.

She rode the elevator down to the parking garage and headed for her car. She was finally done. Done with the job.

Done with Simone.

So why didn't she feel relief? Why did she only feel dread, and anger, and hurt? Everything she'd spent the last week pushing down, not allowing herself to feel, was rising to the surface. She couldn't hold it back much longer. She couldn't keep herself from falling apart. And despite it all, she wished that Simone was there to pick up the pieces and put her back together again, just like she had before.

Jade couldn't turn to Simone any longer. But there was someone else who had been there for her for years and years, even when Jade shut her out. After their fight on Sunday night, they hadn't spoken at all. But if Jade didn't face her friend, she was no better than Simone.

She took out her phone and dialed Renee's number.

"I need to talk to you," she said. "Can I come over?"

Renee opened her front door, her face warped with concern.

"What's the matter?" she asked. "You sounded so upset on the phone."

Had it been that obvious? Jade had been trying so hard to hold herself together, but she was moments from breaking down.

"Hey," Renee put a hand on Jade's shoulder. "Why don't you come in so we can talk?"

Jade nodded. Renee led her inside and sat her down on the couch.

"Do you want something to drink?" Renee asked. "Tea, maybe? Or something stronger?"

Jade shook her head. "You're not mad at me? For Sunday night?"

"Of course not." Renee took a seat next to her. "So we had a little fight. It happens. And I'm sorry again for what I said."

"Don't be. Everything you said is true. I've been a bad friend. I've been so self-absorbed, and I've been pushing you away. I've been pushing everyone away ever since grad school. And it's all because of Philippa."

"What do you mean? Who's Philippa?"

Jade tucked her legs underneath her. "She was my graduate adviser. And she... she took advantage of me."

Drawing in a deep breath, Jade told Renee everything. About her secret relationship with Philippa. About the way Philippa had treated her. About how it had left her so broken that she'd almost dropped out of grad school completely.

"So that's why you disappeared back then?" Renee asked. "That's why you went home and wouldn't tell anyone what was going on? All this time, I thought you'd just burned out from pushing yourself so hard all the time. But it was because of this professor?"

Jade nodded. "I couldn't be around her. I couldn't even be at school. And I couldn't tell anyone what happened because I thought at worst, no one would believe me, and at best, they'd just say it was my fault. I know that it wasn't my fault now, but at the time, I blamed myself. So I kept my mouth shut."

"Shit, Jade. I'm so sorry. I'm sorry you went through all that alone. I'm sorry I wasn't there for you. I tried to be, but I didn't know what was going on. It felt like no matter what I did, I couldn't get through to you, so I just gave up trying."

"It's not your fault. There was nothing you could have done. I was the only one who could dig myself out of that hole. It took me so long to do that. And I never really moved on from it until I met Simone. She made me feel like my old self again. Like I was that girl who moved to LA with stars in my eyes and big dreams." Jade's voice quavered. "But that feeling is gone now. Because Simone, she…"

Renee put her hand on Jade's arm. "What happened?"

Swallowing the lump in her throat, Jade told her about everything that had happened. Her meeting with Philippa. Simone following her and seeing them together. Their confrontation at Club Velvet.

How it had ended with Jade telling her it was over.

"I had to," she said softly. "I had to end it. I couldn't trust her anymore. I couldn't be with someone who would treat me that way. Not again." She felt a hollowness in her chest. "But I still want her. And it hurts so bad."

"Oh, honey." Renee put her arm around Jade's shoulders. "I'm sorry. I know it hurts, but you'll get through this. You're strong, and you're not alone. If you need a shoulder to cry on, or someone to talk to, even just someone to be there, I'm right here, okay?"

"Thanks, Ree."

"Don't sweat it. You'll be all right. And once this is all over, we need to talk about the way you keep setting yourself on fire to keep other people warm. You spent the last week working for Simone after all of that? You have to know how insane that is."

"I know. But she needed me."

"You're a better woman than me." Renee shook her head. "I'm really sorry things didn't work out with Simone. It probably doesn't help to hear this, but after you started seeing her, you seemed happier. Brighter. But I know you'll find someone who makes you feel like that again. Someone who treats you like a princess and shows you all the love you deserve. She's out there waiting for you, I'm sure of it."

But Renee's words rang hollow. Because Jade didn't want someone else.

She only wanted Simone.

CHAPTER 32

"Good evening, gentlemen." Simone slid into her seat. "I apologize for keeping you waiting."

"No worries," Alan, the older of the two men sitting across from her, said. "We went ahead and ordered drinks."

As they exchanged introductions, the men's drinks arrived. Simone ordered herself a glass of wine. She needed it tonight. She'd arrived at the restaurant only ten minutes late, but any amount of lateness was unacceptable. She didn't keep others waiting, didn't play the kind of childish power games some in the business liked to play. She showed everyone the same respect she expected, even her competitors.

But she wasn't meeting with competitors tonight. Alan and Daniel owned an investment firm in New York. With the acquisition of The Star, Los Angeles and the entire West Coast were hers. It was time to think bigger, to expand into the East Coast market. And for that, she needed partners with local contacts and knowledge.

Daniel, the younger of the men, looked around the high-end French restaurant. "What did you do to land a table here? I try to get a reservation every time I'm in LA, but it's booked out a year ahead."

"I have friends in useful places." Simone knew the owner of the restaurant personally. While it was Jade who had made the reservation weeks ago, all it had taken was the mention of Simone's name. She'd even booked Simone's favorite table by the window without being asked.

But Jade wasn't her assistant any longer. She was gone. Gone from the office. Gone from Simone's life. All because Simone had let her doubts poison her.

"If you're as well connected as you seem, this will be a very beneficial partnership for all of us," Daniel said.

Simone swirled her wine around in her glass before raising it to her lips and sipping slowly. "I wouldn't be here if I didn't think so. You're looking for a foothold in Los Angeles, and I can get you one. While hotels are my area of expertise, I like to stay abreast of all local opportunities. I believe you have your eye on commercial real estate downtown?"

"You've done your research," Daniel said.

"I like to know exactly who I'm getting into business with. So let's talk about what we have to offer each other."

Alan took a swig of his whiskey. "Straight to the point." His gaze dipped to Simone's chest before meeting her eyes. "I like that."

Simone kept her face stone, returning Alan's gaze with a steely stare. A slip-up, or a case of wandering eyes? It wouldn't be the first time. She'd spent half her career dealing with leering colleagues and men making crass comments about their female peers. She'd learned long ago how to put said men in their place, making it clear she wouldn't tolerate such behavior without losing her temper. Because in the corporate world, a woman's righteous anger meant being labeled 'difficult,' tanking deals, or worse, tanking her entire career.

It was a delicate line to walk. And while Simone had walked it a thousand times, she didn't enjoy it.

She returned her attention to the meeting at hand. While tonight's dinner was a casual affair, it was just as important as any meeting that took place around a conference room table. So why couldn't she focus?

Why did her mind keep wandering back to Jade?

Jade. Her assistant. Her submissive. The only woman who had ever made her want anything more.

And Simone had pushed her away.

"Are we boring you?" Daniel asked. "Alan can go on and on sometimes, especially after a few drinks."

"Not at all." Simone hadn't heard a word the man said. "Please, continue."

She took another sip of her wine and found her glass almost empty. She was usually careful to keep an eye on how much she was drinking, but she was off her game tonight.

No, not tonight. She'd been off her game ever since Jade had told her it was over. Missing appointments. Turning up late to work. Tuning out during meetings.

It was entirely unlike her. But she couldn't bring herself to care about work, or anything else. She was numb to it all.

And when their appetizers arrived, she didn't hesitate to order another glass of wine, silencing the voice in her head that told her to pace herself. Alan and Daniel shared no such inhibitions. Both men were on to their fourth drink by the time the main course rolled around.

Alan gave the young server a nod as she set down their entrées. "Thanks, doll."

The woman gave him a strained smile. As she walked away, Alan's eyes followed, staring shamelessly at her ass.

"Whew," he whistled. "The ladies in LA are something else. Not like the uptight broads in New York. That hotel you put us up in, right next to the beach, with all those sunbathers? Let me tell you, there are some great views, if you know what I mean."

Simone leaned back in her chair and crossed her arms. "What exactly do you mean, Alan? Please, enlighten me."

Daniel cleared his throat, shooting Alan a sharp look before turning to Simone.

"I've been meaning to ask you about your latest acquisition," he said. "The Ashton Star? No one thought Ashton would ever actually sell that place. Her family has been clinging to it for decades. How did you manage to pull that off?"

A shift in conversation with a side of flattery. Daniel knew how to play the game. Perhaps it was a necessity with a partner like Alan. It was becoming clear that Alan's little slip-up earlier wasn't a slip-up at all. And that he wasn't the kind of person Simone wanted to do business with.

Nevertheless, she entertained the change of subject. "It was a simple matter of understanding where the true value of the hotel lies. The Star is more than the land it was built on. Ashton needed to know that whoever she sold her hotel to understood that."

"An interesting approach. I can see why—"

Daniel's words were interrupted by the ringing of Alan's cell phone. Half the restaurant turned to stare. At such an upscale venue, where ambiance was at a premium, an unsilenced phone was a cardinal sin.

That didn't stop Alan from cursing loudly and taking his phone from his pocket. "It's my assistant. What the hell does she want?" He answered the call, making no attempt to keep his voice down. "What is it? I'm at dinner."

Daniel gave Simone an apologetic look. She took a long swig of her wine. She was quickly reaching the end of her tolerance for Alan.

"Just tell her to call a babysitter," he barked. "Christ, you don't have to call me for every damn thing." He hung up the phone and slipped it into his pocket. "My assistant. I swear to god, I'm one phone call away from firing that girl. She's more trouble than she's worth. Frigid bitch is pissed because she caught me looking at her ass the other day."

"Jesus, Alan!" Daniel turned to Simone. "I'm so sorry. He isn't usually like this. He's had a few too many drinks, that's all."

"Relax, Simone doesn't mind." Alan looked her up and down, licking his lips. "Haven't you heard? She appreciates a good-looking woman as much as any red-blooded man."

Simone placed her glass down on the table. "Oh, I do. But unlike you, I'm not a neanderthal who leers at every woman who crosses his path. Nor do I feel the need to make such vile comments about them."

Alan chuckled. "This right here. This is why you have a reputation for being a stone-cold *bitch*."

Simone's jaw tightened. *Walk the line. Just walk the line like you always do.*

But tonight? She didn't care about walking the line. She didn't care about this deal.

She didn't care if she burned her entire career down.

She took her napkin from her lap and threw it onto the table beside her plate. "We're done here."

Daniel blinked. "I'm sorry?"

"I said, *we're done here.*"

"Lighten up, will you?" Alan said. "It was just a joke."

"A joke?" Simone said. "A joke requires humor, Alan. And there's nothing funny about the misogynistic drivel you've been spewing all evening. You're a pathetic, repulsive man who has no respect for women. And I will not debase myself by working with you."

"Don't be like that," Alan said. "It's just guy talk. You've been in the business long enough to understand that. If you want to play with the big boys, you gotta be able to dish it out *and* take it."

"Perhaps that's how it works in whatever boys' club you run in New York. But here in Los Angeles? I am *queen.*" Simone rose to her feet. "I own half the hotels in this city. I'm better connected than you could ever hope to be. Everyone who's anyone in LA? They'll do whatever I ask them in a heartbeat. So say another word. Say one more *fucking* word. And I will make sure nobody on the entire West Coast ever works with you again."

She looked from one man to the other. Both remained silent.

"Goodbye, gentlemen. Suffice it to say, I'll be looking elsewhere for investors." She nodded to Daniel, who had at least attempted to keep things civil. "Dinner is on me. I wish I could say it was a pleasure, but I'd be lying."

With that, she turned and walked away.

There goes that deal. One that had the potential to be as big as the acquisition of The Star. But Simone didn't feel a shred of regret. She felt nothing at all.

Because none of it mattered. *Nothing* mattered, not anymore. Not after she'd lost the one thing that had made her feel complete for the first time in her life.

She couldn't accept that this was it. She couldn't accept that Jade was gone from her world forever. She couldn't let go of her, not without telling her how she felt.

No, not without *showing* her.

Simone needed more than words. She needed to do something that would prove to Jade, once and for all, that she was the only person who could ever hold Simone's heart.

She took her phone from her purse and dialed the number of a woman who went only by her last name.

"Ashton? We need to talk."

CHAPTER 33

J ade set her laptop down on her bed. Another job
application sent. And, with luck, another interview
secured.

She was taking her time finding a new job. After her
tenure as Simone's assistant had ended, she'd taken a whole
month off for the first time in years. Simone had paid her
generously enough that she wouldn't have to worry about
money for a while. She could take as long as she wanted to
find another job.

Plus, she needed the vacation. Working for Simone
Weiss had been just as taxing as she'd expected. And that
was only the professional side of their relationship. Everything that had happened between them had taken its toll on
her. She'd spent a whole week on the couch watching TV in
her pajamas, Renee checking in on her as often as she could.

But seven days of wallowing was all Jade had allowed
herself. After the week ended, she'd shoved her self-pity
aside and got back on her feet, determined not to fall apart
again. She'd taken a trip to her hometown and spent a week

with her parents, who wouldn't stop gushing about how proud they were of her high-flying life in the big city. She'd spent the next week at a little bed and breakfast down the coast, relaxing and recharging. Then she'd returned to Los Angeles to start her job search.

She'd applied for five jobs so far, and she'd gotten interview offers from all but one. She could hardly believe her luck.

But maybe it wasn't luck. Maybe it was something else.

Jade glanced at the stack of papers on the bed beside her. Right on top was Simone's letter of recommendation.

She picked it up and read over it again. It painted her in the best possible light, a far better light than she deserved. Even now, Simone was still taking care of her.

Longing gripped at her stomach. She'd cried over Simone for what felt like days, then she'd put it all behind her and moved on.

So why did she still miss Simone? Why did she keep reading the letter over and over, just to see her words, to hear her voice in her mind?

Why did she feel like she'd lost a part of herself she'd never known was missing?

Her fingers tightened around the letter, crumpling the corner of the page. She set it down and smoothed it out. *You need to stop thinking about her. You need to get on with your life.*

You need to start living again.

And what better time to do that than now, when her life was flourishing? On top of all the job interviews she had lined up, she'd started looking at new apartments, places with more than one room. She'd replaced her car with a newer, more reliable model. She'd repaired her friendship with Renee, along with a few other friends from college she'd lost touch with over the years. She'd even gotten a call from her grad school's Title IX office telling her that Philippa was under investigation.

Everything was going Jade's way. So why did her life feel more bitter than sweet?

With a sigh, she picked up her laptop again. She wanted to check whether she'd gotten any more messages from recruiters.

But as she opened her inbox, she spotted an email she'd missed earlier. It had been sent in the morning.

And it was from Simone.

Jade's stomach flipped. Why would Simone contact her? She'd sent an email, not a message. That meant it was professional, not personal.

She opened the email. It was an invitation to a press conference at The Ashton Star. With renovations set to begin, the hotel was due to close in a matter of days. But Simone was using The Ashton Star's closure as an opportunity to formally announce her acquisition of the hotel, along with her company's plan for it going forward.

According to the email, the press conference would take place this evening in just a couple of hours. And at the end of the email was a personal note from Simone.

Jade,

You played an important role in making this happen. I couldn't have done it without you. You deserve to be here for this.

And I'd like you to be here too.

Jade's heart skipped. This was the first time Simone had reached out to her since her final day on the job. That had to mean it was important to her.

She read Simone's words again. A request, not a

command. But Jade longed to obey all the same. She longed to see Simone again.

She longed to believe that things could be made right between them.

She closed her eyes. There was no going back to the way things were. No erasing everything that had happened.

But if there was the slightest chance the rift between them could be mended? The slightest sliver of hope?

Jade had to take it.

She shut her laptop, got up from her bed, and started getting ready.

~

Jade arrived at The Ashton Star ten minutes after the press conference had been due to start. She'd left her studio with plenty of time to spare, but a traffic jam meant the drive had taken twice as long as it usually did.

She slipped into the lobby, where the press conference was taking place. It had already begun, but no one noticed her late arrival. Everyone's attention was fixed on the landing of the grand staircase at the center of the room, where Simone stood delivering a speech.

Jade's heart caught in her throat. It was the first time she'd laid eyes on Simone in almost a month. And just a glimpse of her stirred something inside Jade, that same something she'd felt the first time their eyes met at Club Velvet.

She tried to listen to Simone's words, but from her place near the door, she couldn't hear a thing. She made her way forward, edging around the crowd of journalists and photographers until she found a spot to the side. It wasn't the best angle, but there were fewer heads to peer around, and she was close enough to hear Simone clearly.

"Renovations will begin next week," Simone continued as she looked out over the crowd. "And when the hotel reopens in a year's time, it will be transformed into something new, something that embodies the spirit of—"

She stopped short. Because at that moment, her gaze fell upon Jade.

Jade's breath stopped in her chest. For a moment, Simone didn't move, didn't speak. Murmurs broke out in the watching crowd, puzzled glances exchanged.

And when Simone spoke, her eyes didn't leave Jade's.

"When the hotel reopens," Simone said. "It will be a beacon of light in our magnificent city, a shining star that represents the dream Los Angeles stands for. That's why the hotel will reopen as The Jade Star."

Jade blinked. *The Jade Star?*

"Someone very special to me helped bring the dream of The Jade Star to life," Simone said. "And this is for her."

Jade's heart began to pound. But as Simone descended the stairs, her heart stopped completely.

She's coming over here.

The crowd parted before Simone as she strode confidently toward Jade. Cameras flashed, whispers rising around her. But as soon as Simone reached her, they fell silent. All eyes were on the two of them.

"Jade," she said softly. "My brilliant, shining star. My precious jewel. My love. This hotel is dedicated to you."

Jade's stomach fluttered. "Are you saying you... you love me?"

"Yes, Jade. I love you with all my heart. And I want you to be mine."

And just like in so many other moments Jade had shared with her, every thought, every doubt, every worry left her mind. Her body took over. Her *heart* took over.

And her arms were around Simone's neck, pulling her into a deep, tender kiss.

Cameras snapped around them, someone in the crowd nearby letting out a whistle. But Jade barely noticed. The rest of the world had faded away. There was only Simone. The touch of her lips. The press of her body, unwavering, unyielding. The scent of her, as familiar and reassuring as home. Everything she ever wanted—*needed*—was right here in her arms.

Simone broke the kiss and turned to address the crowd. "You'll have to forgive me, but I'm cutting this press conference short. I won't be taking any questions today. You can direct your queries to my assistant. Thank you for coming out."

The crowd dispersed around them, a handful of people saying goodbye to Simone with knowing nods and smiles. And when Ashton approached and offered them her congratulations, Jade couldn't help but blush.

"Was she in on this?" Jade asked once Ashton was gone. "Changing the name of the hotel? She was pretty insistent on you calling it The Star. It was even in the contract."

"That's why I had her amend the contract," Simone said. "She refused at first, but then I told her why. Like I once told you, humans are driven by our emotions, first and foremost. Appealing to Ashton's romantic side was all it took."

"So she knows about us?" Jade glanced around at the photographers packing up their equipment. "I guess everyone knows about us now. Or they will once those photos get out."

"Yes, and I apologize for putting you on the spot. I didn't plan it, but when I saw you in the crowd, looking up at me, I had to seize the chance to tell you how I felt, to say the words I've wanted to say to you for so long." She took Jade's hands in hers. "I've said it before, but I'm sorry for hurting you. I can't undo that. What I can do is promise you I'll never do anything to hurt you again. And I'll do everything in my power to keep you from hurting."

"I know you will. And I need to apologize too. After having some time to think about it, I understand why you reacted the way you did, especially with everything you've been through. So I'm sorry too. And Simone?"

"Yes?"

"I love you, too."

Simone drew her in and kissed her again, gentle, soft, and slow. As Jade dissolved into her lips, her heart sang.

It was finally whole again.

CHAPTER 34

Simone stepped through her front door and shut it behind her. "Jade?" she called. "I'm home."

As she hung up her coat, Jade appeared, greeting her with a fiery kiss.

"Someone is in a good mood this evening," Simone murmured. "I take it your first day at your new job went well?"

"It went great." Jade took her hand and pulled her over to the couch, drawing her down onto it. "It's a little different from working for you. The company is huge, and I'm reporting to the whole executive team, not just the CEO. But there are lots of opportunities to advance my career. If I play my cards right, I might make Chief of Staff, eventually."

"I'm glad the job is working out," Simone said.

"Well, it isn't all sunshine and roses. The VP is a real hardass. Everyone is afraid of him. Not me though. I can handle it." A playful grin spread across Jade's lips. "After all, I spent three months working for Simone Weiss."

"And you did an excellent job of it, too. I have half a

mind to steal you back and have you come work for me again." She draped her arm around Jade's shoulders. "But I'd only hold you back. You're meant for far bigger things. And as you chase those dreams, I'll be right here to support you however I can."

Jade let out a contented sigh. "I could never have asked for a better girlfriend. Honestly, I still can't believe this is real. That I get to be with you, and we don't have to sneak around. That we get to live together. That I get to fall asleep next to you every night."

Moving in together had been the natural next step for them. Jade had already been looking at new apartments, so Simone had suggested she move into her Beverly Hills home with her instead. Jade hadn't hesitated to accept her offer.

"I have the perfect girlfriend," she said. "The perfect job. The perfect life. It's like some kind of dream."

Simone traced her fingers down Jade's arm. "If this is a dream, I never want to wake up."

Jade leaned against her shoulder, nestling into her. But after a few seconds, she sat up straight, her fingers fidgeting in her lap.

"I almost forgot," she said. "I have news. It's about Philippa."

Simone tensed. Just the sound of the woman's name was enough to set her on edge.

But she kept her voice calm. "Did you finally hear back from your grad school?"

Jade nodded. "Up until now, all they've been able to tell me is that the issue is under investigation. But I got a call today from the person handling the case. She said that the reason things have taken so long is because another student already reported her. A *current* student. And my report on top of hers was enough to push the school to take things seriously. Between the two of us, they have enough evidence to take action against Philippa. She's been fired from her job. And with everything on record, she'll never get another teaching position again."

"That's wonderful news. How are you feeling about it?"

"Good, I think. This has all been pretty stressful, so it's a relief to finally have some kind of resolution. I'm just glad she's faced justice."

"And all because of you." Simone took Jade's hand, lacing her fingers through hers. "I know none of this has been easy, but you've been braver than anyone could hope to be. *You* made this happen. You should be proud of yourself."

"It wasn't all me. It was you who gave me the push I needed to make that choice. And not just to face Philippa and tell people what she did. The choice to move forward. The choice to open my heart again."

"And I'm happy you did. Because having you in my life, having you as mine, means the world to me. I love you more than words can describe."

"I will never get tired of hearing you say that," Jade purred.

Simone leaned in and kissed her. Jade wrapped her arms around Simone's neck, deepening the kiss, drawing her closer. Desire stirred inside her as Jade's body melted against hers, pliant, soft, and eager.

She murmured into Simone's lips, drawing back slightly. "I've been thinking, and I..." Jade glanced away before meeting her eyes again. "I'm ready. You know, to try what we talked about."

Simone studied her face. "Are you sure?"

Jade nodded. Ever since they got back together, they'd spent every spare moment exploring their desires, discovering new depths of intimacy, even pushing their limits. They'd come to trust each other enough now to take those steps.

"I think you're ready too," Simone said. "You're certain this is what you want?"

"I am," Jade replied. "I want to do this. I was thinking we could do it tonight."

"You have no idea how tempting that is. But are you forgetting I have plans tonight? I'm meeting with the others at Club Velvet."

"Do you really have to go?" Jade traced a finger down Simone's arm, peering up at her from under her eyelashes. "Maybe I can convince you to stay?"

Simone gave her a firm look. "Try it, and I'll have you kneel at the foot of the bed naked the entire time I'm gone."

Jade bit her lip, her eyes betraying the thoughts in her mind.

"Oh?" Simone raised an eyebrow. "Don't tell me the idea is turning you on?"

The flush rising up Jade's face was the only confirmation she needed. After all this time, Simone was still discovering new buttons to push to make her quiver and blush. It never ceased to delight her. And it affirmed what she already knew—that she and Jade were made for each other. Simone wanted to be with her for the rest of her days.

Once upon a time, the thought alone would have been enough to make her put up her guard. She'd never had any faith in relationships, let alone marriage. But with Jade? She wanted that forever. And perhaps, one day, they would take that step.

In the meantime, there was another, smaller step they needed to take in their relationship.

"You know what?" Simone said. "You should come with me tonight."

Jade blinked. "You mean, to Club Velvet?"

"Yes. I want to show you off. Not only to the world, but to the people most important to me." After all, the friends Simone owned Club Velvet with were the closest thing she had to family.

She leaned in, sliding her hand up Jade's thigh as she spoke into her ear.

"And afterward," she said, "if you're good, we can have a little fun, just the two of us. What do you say?"

A smile spread on Jade's lips. "I would love that."

Simone placed her hand on the small of Jade's back. "Everyone, I'd like you to meet my girlfriend, Jade."

She looked around the VIP lounge, where the other owners were gathered. All three women stared back at her, speechless.

Finally, Valerie gave Jade a warm smile. "I'm Valerie. Or Madame V, depending on the time of day. It's a pleasure to meet you."

Her words opened the floodgates. Elle stood up and grabbed Jade's hands, dragging her over to the lounges where the others sat.

"We've been waiting so long to meet you," she said. "I'm Elle, by the way. This is Olivia."

"Olivia De Leon." She held out her hand for Jade to

shake. "So you're the woman who has Simone so infatuated."

"Tell me about it," Elle said. "Simone has been crazy about you since the day you met. She's not the type to shout it from the rooftops, but it was obvious to me."

"Why don't you take a seat?" Valerie gestured to the seat next to her, then nodded at the table before them. It held two bottles of champagne on ice and half a dozen champagne flutes. "When Simone told us she was bringing you, we ordered some champagne to mark the occasion. Would you like a glass?"

Jade sat down next to her. "Sure."

Valerie popped the cork and poured five glasses, handing one to Jade. "This should help you survive Elle's interrogation."

Elle shot her a look before taking one of the champagne flutes from the table and sitting down on the other side of Jade. "I'm not going to interrogate her. But I *am* curious to know what kind of woman managed to capture Simone Weiss's heart."

Jade gave her a sheepish shrug. "I'm nobody special. I guess I got lucky."

"That's where you're wrong." Simone plucked the final glass of champagne from the table, her gaze locked on Jade. "You're more than special. You're a beautiful, intelligent, brilliant woman who takes my breath away every time I look at you. And I'm lucky to call you mine."

"Christ," Olivia murmured. "Keep this up and you'll make me wish I wasn't single."

Simone took a seat across from her girlfriend. Jade was taking the attention in her stride. But the night had only just begun.

"So," Elle said, "what was it like dating Simone while you were working for her at the same time?"

"It wasn't easy," Jade replied. "Especially at first, when we were trying to keep everything outside work. But that didn't last long."

"Oh? So the two of you were sneaking around the office, having a little illicit fun?" Elle gave Jade a knowing look. "Is that big vintage desk Simone loves so much as strong as it looks?"

Jade's cheeks flushed crimson. "T-that's... We never..."

"For your information, we never did anything *on* my desk," Simone said.

"Oh?" Elle leaned toward Jade, a mischievous smile on her lips. "There's one other thing I'd like to know. Does Simone use her disappointed schoolteacher voice in the bedroom too?"

"Elle," Valerie warned. "Stop torturing the girl."

"What? I'm just being friendly. And you can't blame me for being curious. How long have you two been together now? We've been dying to meet you, but Simone has been keeping you to herself."

"Are you surprised?" Valerie said. "You're giving Jade the third degree. It's no wonder Simone wasn't in a hurry to introduce you."

"Is that your excuse for keeping your love life secret from us too, Val?" Elle asked.

"I don't know what you're talking about."

"Sure you don't." Elle crossed her legs and took a sip of her champagne. "So, how's that new nanny of yours doing?"

"Fine," Valerie replied. "Why do you ask?"

"Has she met Madame V yet?"

"Why would she?"

Elle raised an eyebrow. "Really? You're still pretending there's nothing going on there?"

Valerie folded her arms across her chest. "I'm not pretending. Because there *is* nothing going on there."

"Oh please, you always make that face when you're lying."

Jade flattened herself into her seat as the two women argued across her. Simone gave her an apologetic look. At the very least, she was getting the authentic experience of Simone's friends.

Eventually, Olivia steered the conversation back to Jade with some questions about her new job. It wasn't until an hour and another bottle of champagne later that everyone's curiosity had been satisfied and Jade was given a chance to breathe. And soon, Valerie announced that she needed to get home.

She said her goodbyes and disappeared downstairs. As Olivia and Elle fell into a conversation about an upcoming play party at the club, Simone drew Jade over to a quiet corner.

"There you have it," she said. "You've met my friends."

"They seem…" Jade paused in thought.

"Intense?"

"*Nice* is what I was going to say. But that too."

"I'm glad you like them. I'm sure they feel the same about you."

Jade took Simone's hand in hers. "Thank you for bringing me here to meet them tonight."

"The time was right. I am meeting your family in a few weeks, after all."

"I can't wait. My parents are going to love you. If you can win Renee over, you can win over anyone."

"I think it was the Club Velvet VIP membership I gave her that won her over."

"Maybe. She's definitely making good use of it."

Simone wrapped her arm around Jade's waist, drawing her in close. Jade, her jewel. Jade, her prize. A treasure more precious than anything else.

And she was all Simone's.

She leaned in, her voice dropping low. "Now that everyone else is occupied, why don't we go take a look at the private rooms? We haven't been back in a long time. We can pick up where we left off at home. And you might just get your wish to try what we talked about earlier."

Jade gazed up at her, desire shimmering in her eyes.

"Whatever you want," she said. "I'm all yours."

CHAPTER 35

"**K**eep moving about like that," Simone said, "and I'll turn you around and spank that pretty ass of yours pink."

Jade froze in place. They'd returned to the room Simone had taken her into the second night she'd gone back to Club Velvet. Some of the equipment from before had been taken to other private rooms, but the bed and the floor-to-ceiling shelves filled with kinky delights had remained. So had the big, X-shaped St Andrews cross.

Which Simone was strapping Jade to right now.

She buckled the final strap around Jade's ankle, sweeping a hand up her leg. "Now there's no way you can wriggle your way out of this."

Heat rose to Jade's skin. Spreadeagled, her arms and legs bound and her body stretched to the limit, she could barely move. And Simone had stripped her down to her panties before strapping her to the cross, leaving her even more vulnerable.

But Simone had stripped down to her bra and panties,

too. And the sight of her, her flushed breasts, her milky white hips and thighs bared for Jade's eyes only, was just as breathtaking as the first time she laid eyes on Simone's body.

But tonight, the sight wasn't to last.

Simone examined the array of blindfolds displayed on the shelf nearby and picked one up, dangling it from a finger. It was made of black leather overlaid with lace, which did little to make it seem less imposing.

"Close your eyes," Simone said.

Jade's pulse sped up, nerves and excitement warring inside her. Once upon a time, blindfolds had been a hard limit. Then, they'd turned into a soft limit. Because the more she and Simone explored, the more the trust between them had grown. And the more Jade had come to understand her fears.

Blindfolds didn't scare her because they made her vulnerable. She'd made herself vulnerable to Simone a thousand times in a thousand different ways. No, her anxiety over blindfolds stemmed from something deeper—her fear of unknowingly being taken advantage of while blind, vulnerable, trusting, just like she had been before.

It was a fear she'd held onto for far too long. It was one she wanted to conquer.

Still, she couldn't help but hesitate.

Simone cupped Jade's cheek in her hand. "You can do this. I know you can. And if you start to feel overwhelmed, I'm right here, understand?"

Jade nodded. Taking a deep breath, she shut her eyes.

"I'm going to put the blindfold on you now," Simone said. "Just relax."

She slipped the blindfold onto Jade's head, taking care

not to tangle the straps in her hair. It fit snugly, the leather unexpectedly soft against her skin. And when she opened her eyes, not a single ray of light reached them.

Her breath quickened. She was completely in the dark.

Simone drew the backs of her fingers down the side of Jade's face. "Deep breaths. Listen to my voice."

Jade closed her eyes under the blindfold again, breathing in and out, drinking Simone in, savoring her scent and the feel of her fingers against her skin. Jade didn't need to see her to feel her presence. She was right there with her.

And with Simone by her side, Jade had nothing to fear.

"Yes, just like that," Simone said, her breath whispering against Jade's skin. "The more you let go, the more wonderful this will feel."

She pressed her lips to Jade's in a brief, lingering kiss. Jade quivered. Had Simone's lips always been so soft and sweet?

"As you'll soon find out for yourself," Simone said, "blindfolds enhance sensation. In taking away your sight, all your other senses are heightened. Just the slightest touch can feel *divine*."

She traced her fingertips down Jade's neck, her collarbone, her breasts, skimming them over a nipple. Jade murmured softly, her chest arching into Simone's touch.

"Every little sensation is magnified," Simone said. "Pleasure, and *pain*."

She took Jade's nipple between her fingertips, pinching it firmly, sending a dart of pleasure through her. But not a moment later, Simone's fingers were replaced by something hard and firm.

Nipple clamps. They'd been a limit once upon a time, too. Not anymore.

Simone clamped the other nipple, then gave the chain between them a tug. Jade sucked in a sharp breath, each clamp a burning kiss on her nipples.

Simone pulled on the chain again. "Does that feel good, princess?"

Jade's head rolled back, her whole body trembling. "So good…"

Simone snaked her hand down Jade's stomach, into the waistband of her silk panties, fingers sliding between her outspread thighs. "You're already so wet for me. Let me show you."

Simone's hand disappeared. A moment later, she pressed her fingers against Jade's lips.

"I want you to feel how wet you are," she said. "I want you *to taste* it."

She slipped two fingers into Jade's mouth. Jade sucked them obediently, tasting her own arousal, slick and sweet and fragrant all at the same time.

Simone withdrew her fingers, trailing them down Jade's chin and throat. "Now you know how good you taste," she said. "Now, it's my turn to taste you."

She ran her hands down Jade's sides, all the way to her panties. Jade's body throbbed. She was desperate for Simone to pull her panties down, to touch her where she needed her the most. But with Jade's legs bound and spread out wide, how could Simone take her panties off?

Suddenly, they tightened around her hips, digging into her flesh as the telltale sound of fabric tearing echoed through the room. Then the tension around her hips was gone, along with her panties. Simone had ripped them clean off.

Jade gasped. But Simone took her surprise as protest, spanking her on the side of her ass.

"I bought these for you, so they're mine. I can do whatever I want with them." Simone drew her hand down Jade's side, following the curve of her waist. "Just like I can with you."

Jade's heart raced. Simone glided her hands down, grabbing hold of her hips. It wasn't until Jade felt the tickle of Simone's breath on the insides of her thighs that she realized Simone had gotten to her knees.

Jade's breath hitched, anticipation sizzling inside her. Until finally, Simone dove between Jade's thighs.

She let out a trembling moan, her body shivering with delight as Simone's lips danced over her folds. Her tongue dipped into Jade's entrance, circling and swirling before sweeping up to her clit. Simone stroked and licked, teasing Jade's swollen bud with the tip of her tongue, sending jolts of electricity through her.

And when she wrapped her lips around it and sucked, it sent a tremor through Jade's body that would have brought her to her knees if she hadn't been held upright by the cross.

"Oh, Simone," she cried. "Oh!"

Her orgasm hit her like a tidal wave, crashing through her body. Her back and hips arched, her arms and legs straining against her bonds. But Simone was relentless, holding onto Jade's hips, her tongue and lips flicking, until every drop of pleasure had left Jade's body.

Jade slumped back against the cross, breathless, but not spent. Somehow, she'd only become hungry for more. So when Simone clawed her way up Jade's stomach and chest, smothering her lips with a kiss that was tinged with the scent of her own arousal, Jade returned it greedily, her body pushing back against Simone's.

Simone purred with satisfaction. "Insatiable as always. But I'm not done with you yet. I brought a little something from home to give you. But first, let's get you off this."

One by one, she unfastened the straps around Jade's arms and legs, leaving her blindfolded but freed from the cross. Then she took Jade by the hand, drawing her to the other end of the room.

"Here," Simone said. "I'm going to lay you down on the bed now."

Slowly, carefully, she guided Jade onto the mattress before her. Jade stretched out along it, waiting for Simone to join her. Instead, her footsteps receded, leaving Jade alone on the bed.

Jade held back a groan. She was still wearing the nipple clamps. Without any other sensations to distract her, their bite was as infuriating as it was delicious.

Finally, Simone's footsteps returned, stopping beside the bed. The mattress swayed as she climbed onto it, settling beside Jade and drawing her hands down her breasts to the clamps at her nipples.

She pulled them off, one after the other, leaving behind a numb tingling that only made Jade hotter. Then she traced her fingertips over the blindfold covering Jade's eyes.

"Keep this on for me," she said. "I want you to really feel this. I want you to really feel me."

She nudged Jade onto her side and slipped into place behind her, kissing her way up Jade's shoulder, her neck, behind her ear. Desire trickled down Jade's back, spreading through her whole body. With her sight taken away, her other senses were magnified, just like Simone had told her. And Simone's touch, her kiss, felt heavenly.

Simone pulled her in closer, her now bare breasts pressing into Jade's back. And lower down, something hard and smooth pressed against her tailbone, sliding down between her legs.

Need flared in Jade's core. The 'little something' Simone had brought from home for her was far from *little*.

She ground back against Simone desperately. "I want you inside me so bad."

"All right, princess," Simone said. "I'll give you what you need."

She took the strap-on, positioning the tip at Jade's entrance. Slowly, she slipped it inside, burying herself deep.

A gasp rose from Jade's chest, pleasure flooding through her. She was so sensitive from her orgasm. But at the same time, it had primed her body for more. And when Simone began to move inside her, her gasps turned to moans, her shivers turning to tremors.

"Yes," Jade whispered. "God, yes…"

She rocked her hips in time with Simone, reaching back blindly to grasp onto her thigh. Her fingers dug into supple flesh, holding on against the tide of pleasure. She whimpered softly, urging Simone on just as much as she wanted to slow her down. She wanted this to last. She wanted to stay in this embrace, skin against skin, Simone deep inside her, for as long as she could.

But she was hurtling ever closer to oblivion. And when Simone reached around and slipped a hand between Jade's thighs to rub her swollen clit, she couldn't fight it any longer.

"Go on," Simone crooned, her lips caressing Jade's ear. "Come for me."

That was all it took to make her come apart for the second time that night. A cry rose from Jade's lips as an orgasm overtook her, rippling through her entire body. Simone thrust and stroked, drawing Jade's orgasm on and on, keeping her suspended in a state of bliss for what felt like an eternity.

And even as Jade's climax faded, Simone didn't stop. Not until she shuddered in her own release, the cry from her chest vibrating through Jade's body and the entire room.

They collapsed back onto the bed, a tangle of limbs, their thirst sated. It was only after Simone had caught her breath that she removed the blindfold from Jade's head.

Simone took Jade's face in her hands, affection simmering in her eyes. "You did so well, princess. How do you feel?"

"Incredible," Jade murmured. "I don't know why I was so afraid to try that."

"I knew you could handle it," Simone said.

"Only because you were there to guide me through it."

Simone drew her into her arms. "And that's where I'll always be. Right here with you."

Simone kissed her gently. Jade sighed into her lips, her chest filling with warmth. As she dissolved into Simone's body, she let go of it all, let the world fade away.

And she lost herself in Simone.

EPILOGUE

J ade hooked her arm through Simone's, resting her head on her shoulder. "Tonight was amazing. This is officially the best anniversary ever."

"We've only had two so far," Simone said.

"And this one was even better than the last."

It had been a day to remember. They'd started with breakfast in bed, which had inevitably led to a lazy morning of exploring each other's bodies like it was the very first time. They'd had a late lunch at Jade's favorite beachside cafe before going for a long walk through the hills, where they'd stopped at an overlook to watch the sun setting over the city. They'd capped off the evening with dinner at Simone's favorite French restaurant, which had become one of Jade's favorites too.

And at long last, they were on their way home.

"The night isn't over yet," Simone said. "I may have told a little lie about where we're going next."

Jade glanced up at her. "What do you mean?"

"We're not going home tonight. I have one last surprise for you."

Hm? Jade peered out the car window. They were nowhere near Beverly Hills. She hadn't even noticed.

Where was Simone taking her?

But her question was answered when they pulled into the circular driveway in front of a familiar building.

"Here we are," Simone said. "The Jade Star."

The car stopped at the entrance to the hotel, a white-gloved valet materializing to open the passenger door. Jade slid out of the car and onto the red carpet, gazing up at the hotel. Now, The Jade Star was as familiar to her as the home she shared with Simone. But it still took her breath away.

It would always be special to them. And not only because Simone had given it Jade's name. Since the day she acquired the hotel, Simone had poured her heart and soul into it. And now, it was thriving. Now, it was the brightest star in Los Angeles.

Simone joined her by the entrance, slipping her hand into Jade's. "Shall we?"

Together, they stepped through the doors. Jacques greeted them warmly before leading them to the penthouse elevator and pressing the call button for them. Mercifully, he didn't insist on accompanying them up to the suite. But Jade didn't miss the nod he gave Simone as the elevator doors slid closed.

Jade's stomach skittered. They'd spent the night in the penthouse suite a dozen times before. So why the fanfare? What was waiting for her in the penthouse? There was nothing that could make her night any better. Nothing that could make the life she shared with Simone any better. She was climbing the ladder at her job, having been promoted twice in two years. Simone had expanded her hotel empire to the East Coast, just like she'd planned. Club Velvet had recently celebrated its second anniversary and was still going strong.

And Jade's relationship with Simone? It grew stronger every day.

Finally, the elevator reached the top floor. The doors opened, revealing the familiar suite. But as Jade stepped out of the elevator, she found the floor beneath her feet covered in rose petals, forming a trail that led through the living room, all the way to the bedroom. And flanking either side of the trail was a row of tea lights.

Jade brought her hand to her chest, turning to Simone. "Did you do this?"

Simone nodded. "Go on. Follow it."

Jade followed the trail to the bedroom, Simone a step behind her. Inside, it continued onto the bed, fanning out over the sheets in a shower of rose petals.

"Simone," she said. "This is just…"

But as Jade turned around to face her, her heart stopped. Simone had gotten down on one knee, a small velvet box in her hand. Inside was a ring, gold with an elaborate arrangement of sparkling diamonds.

"Jade," she began. "From the moment I met you, all I wanted was to make you mine. What I never expected was that I'd fall for you so deeply. With every precious moment we spent together, you captured a piece of my heart. Until one day, I realized that every part of it, every part of *me*, belonged to you. I'm yours. I always will be. That's why I'm asking you for one more gift."

Jade's lips parted, but not a single sound came out. Not even a breath.

"Jade Fisher," Simone said. "Will you give me the gift of forever? Will you give me the gift of being my wife?"

Jade's heart surged. "Yes. Simone, *yes*."

Jade fell to her knees and threw her arms around her. As Simone pressed her lips to Jade's, salty tears spilled into her mouth. Were they hers, or Simone's? What did it matter now that the two of them would become one?

Jade broke the kiss, but didn't let go of Simone. "We're getting married. This is really happening."

A smile crossed Simone's lips. "I think this calls for a celebration, don't you?"

"Definitely. What did you have in mind?"

Simone rose to her feet and held out her hand. "Come with me and you'll find out."

Jade stood up and took her hand. But instead of leading her to the petal-covered bed, Simone led her to the bathroom and opened the door. Inside, the bathtub was filled to the brim, the scent of jasmine hanging in the air. A dozen candles cast a soft light around the room, a bench beside the bath holding a bottle of champagne and a platter of fruit and chocolate.

Simone slipped behind her and wrapped her arms around Jade's waist. "Here's what we're going to do. We're going to get into this luxurious bath. We're going to enjoy this delicious spread. And then, we'll go back into the bedroom and I'll make sure that tonight truly is a night you'll never forget. How does that sound, princess?"

Jade turned her head, planting a soft kiss on Simone's lips. "It sounds perfect."

ABOUT THE AUTHOR

Anna Stone is the author of lesbian romance bestsellers Being Hers, Tangled Vows, and more. Her sizzling sapphic romances feature strong, passionate women who love women. In every one of her books, you'll find off-the-charts heat and a guaranteed happily ever after.

Anna lives in Australia with her girlfriend and their cat. When she isn't writing, she can usually be found with a coffee in one hand and a book in the other.

Visit **annastoneauthor.com** to find out more about her books and to sign up for her newsletter.

Printed in Great Britain
by Amazon

38849359R00158